# Olivia's Choice

*Thomas Kelly*

# Olivia's Choice

*By Thomas Kelly*

For Kathy

# Prologue
## *Coming to America*

Gabriela Rossi, an adventuresome sixteen-year-old with a bright smile, arrived in New York City in the fall of 1914 with her parents and younger brother, Mario. She was one of three million Italian immigrants who journeyed to the United States between 1900 and 1915.

The only job Gabriela could find was working in a sewing factory that specialized in women's blouses. Most of the workers were teenagers, Jewish and Italian immigrants who spoke little to no English.

Crowded together in a dimly lit factory, they sat on uncomfortable chairs that had no backs. After just a few hours on her first day, Gabriela's neck and back ached terribly as she stitched on her machine. Her body gradually acclimated to the conditions, but when she left the factory each day, she took the pain home with her.

Gabriela made seven dollars a week, working nine hours a day on weekdays and six hours on Saturdays.

After four arduous years at the sewing factory, she was thrilled when a generous Italian couple hired her as a nanny. Their four children, ages seven to one, could be challenging, but she quickly came to love the entire family.

Even her hardest days caring for the children were more enjoyable than her best days at the sewing factory.

On a spring morning in 1920, Gabriela was navigating a crowded sidewalk when a young man bumped into her. He'd been reading while walking when the book fell from his hands.

"I'm sorry," he said, sheepishly retrieving his book from the dingy ground.

1

"Walking and reading do not go well together, especially here in Manhattan," she said with a grin.

The young man, a Utah native, could tell from her accent that she was Italian. He was drawn to her pleasant smile. A self-proclaimed bookworm, he'd bumped into countless people on the street since arriving in the city to study medicine six years earlier. But he'd never before felt like chatting with one of them.

As Gabriela continued down the street, he ran to catch up. They walked together for a couple of blocks before he summoned the courage to invite her to join him in Central Park.

"I'd be happy to, as long as you promise not to bring a book."

"Cross my heart," he replied. "My name is Aaron, by the way."

"Pleasure to meet you, Aaron. I'm Gabriela."

Two days later, they walked hand in hand through the park under a flawless sky. She told him that while she loved living in America, her parents missed Rome and the many family members who still lived there.

Spurred by memories of home, Gabriela began singing in Italian. Aaron didn't understand the words, but the purity of her voice was mesmerizing.

"You're a natural," he said. "I could listen to you all day."

She smiled. "Thanks. I love to sing."

Aaron and Gabriela began seeing each other several times a week. She found his smile strikingly attractive and he loved her zest for life.

One evening after work, Gabriela was rushing to catch a streetcar when she noticed a distraught elderly woman. A thief had just stolen the woman's purse. Gabriela gently took her by the hand and walked the remaining six blocks until they reached the humble apartment where the woman lived alone. Before leaving, Gabriela gave the woman all the money she had in her own purse. It was nearly every cent of the nine dollars she earned that week as a nanny.

The woman kissed Gabriela on each cheek and tearfully thanked her for the kind gesture. Because she had no money left for a streetcar, Gabriela spent the next two hours walking back to her family's apartment.

Aaron soon became a regular Sunday dinner guest in the Rossi's small apartment. He always brought gifts: fruit or flowers for Gabriela's mother and chocolate for her father, whose sweet tooth was legendary. Her parents always greeted him with a kiss on each cheek.

Aaron was thoroughly smitten. He adored Gabriela with all his heart and savored the moments they spent together. Her journey took a slightly slower pace. Three months after they first met, she told Aaron that she loved him.

2

Gabriela began attending the Church of Jesus Christ of Latter-day Saints with Aaron. She read from the Book of Mormon and prayed to know of its truth. Though her testimony quickly flourished, she proceeded at the deliberate pace she was accustomed to. Eight months later, Aaron baptized and confirmed her a member of the Church of Jesus Christ of Latter-day Saints.

Shortly thereafter, they exchanged wedding vows in a small ceremony in New York. Their goal was to be sealed in an LDS temple, so they carefully saved enough money to travel to the nearest temple, which was in Utah.

Misfortune struck the Rossi family when Gabriela's father lost his job. Nearly a year later, he still hadn't found employment. The family was drowning financially and his sense of self-worth likewise plummeted.

Gabriela's mom prayed fervently that someone would throw her discouraged husband a lifeline. And, eventually, someone did. A prosperous cousin in Rome offered Gabriela's father a job, which would require him to return to Italy. The decision to leave America was heartbreaking for Gabriela's parents and brother, but they were convinced it was the right thing to do. Even after eight years in America, they still felt like strangers in a strange land.

Soon after Gabriela bid her family a tearful farewell, she and Aaron learned the news that they were expecting. On November 8, 1922, she delivered identical twin girls. They named them Angela and Maria.

Aaron would always remember that sacred day when he first held his daughters in his arms. The connection was immediate. Although he was just meeting them, he already loved them with all his heart.

Watching his baby girls through the nursery window, Aaron reflected on his many roles: husband, father, son, brother, friend, physician. His own life felt unmistakably different now that they'd experienced the miracle of bringing two new lives into this world.

In 1925, Aaron and Gabriela decided to move west with their daughters. Their first destination was the Salt Lake Temple, where the family was sealed for eternity. They continued on to Savona Springs, a growing city in southern California in desperate need of a physician. The city continued to prosper until the Great Depression swept across the country in 1929. As unemployment rose to heartbreaking levels, many of Aaron's patients could no longer pay for his services, though he never turned anyone away.

Aaron and Gabriela often prayed that they'd be able to have a third child, but it was not to be.

When Angela and Maria graduated from high school in 1940, their parents were left wondering how time had flown by so quickly. That fall, the twins started attending Savona Springs University, where they both majored in nursing.

On Sunday, December 7, 1941, the family was returning from church when nearly every radio in town began broadcasting the news that Japan had attacked Pearl Harbor. The unprovoked act of war killed more than 2,400 people and ushered the United States into the nightmare of World War II.

Life changed dramatically. Common items such as wool, shoes, sugar, cheese, and bicycles were subject to rationing. The speed limit was lowered to thirty-five miles per hour, which was referred to as "Victory Speed," because it conserved gasoline and rubber needed for the military.

Brimming with patriotism, Angela and Maria both wanted to serve as U.S. Army nurses after graduating from college. They planned to attend school year-round so they could complete their degrees in August of 1943.

One day, Angela read the heartbreaking story of the Sullivan family in Iowa. They had five sons and one daughter. All five boys decided to join the Navy after the attack on Pearl Harbor and were assigned together to the USS Juneau in the Pacific. In November of 1942, a Japanese torpedo struck the Juneau and the ship was lost. The Sullivans awaited word regarding their sons' safety, paralyzed with fear because all letters had ceased following the attack.

Finally, on a freezing winter day the following January, three uniformed men appeared at the Sullivan home.

"I'm very sorry, but we are here with news for you," said the ranking officer.

"Which one?" Mr. Sullivan asked, grabbing his heart.

"I'm so sorry," replied the officer. "All five."

After learning about the loss of the Sullivan brothers, Angela and Maria began to worry greatly about their own parents. If the girls both died while serving as nurses, their parents would have no living children and no hope of grandchildren.

When the two sisters prayed for guidance, Angela felt prompted that she and Maria should talk with Professor Jane Hall, the head of the College of Nursing. In addition to being the twins' favorite teacher, Professor Hall had served valiantly during World War I as an Army nurse in France.

"You know both of us better than just about anyone," Angela said to Professor Hall. "And you know what it's like to be a wartime nurse. In your opinion, which one of us is better suited to serve?"

Professor Hall told Angela and Maria that she wanted to talk to each of them separately before answering their question. After she'd spoken with both sisters, she spent an hour in her office alone. She then invited Angela and Maria to join her. As Professor Hall spoke, the twins held hands. Though they wanted to be brave, both trembled.

"Each of you desperately tried to convince me that you were better suited for military service than your sister," said Professor Hall as tears filled her eyes. "It was clear to me what you were doing. You wanted to protect your sister from the horrors of war. You placed her safety above your own. Your selfless love for each other has touched me deeply."

Professor Hall paused for a moment. "I've reached my decision," she finally said. "You would both be excellent nurses. But I feel that Angela's temperament is best suited to the incredible stress of war."

Since Angela and Maria had previously agreed to follow Professor Hall's recommendation, the final decision had been made. Maria became a full-time nurse at Lakeside Hospital in Savona Springs after graduation. Angela crossed the Atlantic Ocean on her way to Anzio, Italy, 35 miles south of Rome, the Eternal City.

The Army couldn't have sent Angela to a more dangerous place.

# Chapter 1
## *The Girl in the Purple Sweater*

Anthony Hull looked from the airport terminal to the Boeing 767 that would soon take him from Savona Springs to New York City, where his best friend was getting married the following day.

Anthony was, without a doubt, the best player on the Savona Springs University basketball team. Though he was generously listed on the roster as six feet tall, he had long arms and quick reflexes. His shooting touch was exceptional, and he averaged twenty-six points per game. A local television station had recently held a contest to give Anthony a nickname. "The Incredible Hull" won in a landslide.

Anthony took his place at the end of a long line of passengers waiting to board the plane. He noticed a beautiful girl wearing a purple sweater standing a short distance ahead. She was talking intently on her phone. Even from a distance, Anthony noticed how kind her voice sounded.

The girl looked in his direction, allowing Anthony to observe her most striking feature – her stunning green eyes. They were big and bright and beautiful.

Although Anthony stared at her, the girl in the purple sweater barely noticed. Olivia Michaels was on her way to England for a weeklong vacation with her parents. A week earlier, she'd graduated from BYU and returned to Savona Springs, where she'd been born and raised.

After passing through airport security that morning, Olivia had received an emotional call from Rachel Ryan, her missionary trainer and best friend. Rachel cried as she told Olivia that her fiancé was thinking of calling off their wedding because he'd come down with a bad case of cold feet.

While listening to her friend, Olivia had stopped at a popular airport eatery called Happy Landings. She ordered a breakfast burrito because they looked so delicious on the menu. When her food arrived, however, it looked more like a soggy paper towel roll. She managed to force down a few bites, then took an ibuprofen tablet. She had a sprained ankle that was beginning to throb due to a busy morning of being on her feet.

Olivia continued her call with Rachel as she made her way to the boarding gate. Her parents soon joined her in line. When it was her turn to give her boarding pass to the gate agent, Olivia suddenly realized that she didn't have her purse. With a look of pure panic in her eyes, she told the agent, "I think I left my purse at a restaurant. My boarding pass and passport are in it. I'll run and get it right now."

"You don't have time," said the gate agent without a trace of sympathy in her voice. "The plane leaves in a few minutes. We can't hold it just for you."

Olivia felt sick to her stomach. *This can't be happening.*

"I'll get your purse," a friendly voice said. It was Anthony.

She turned around and exclaimed, "My purse is on a chair near the back of Happy Landings. It has blue and white stripes."

Anthony took off at a full sprint, weaving in and out of the crowd to avoid bumping into other travelers. *Wow, he's really fast,* Olivia thought as he disappeared around a corner. She was astonished that a stranger would risk missing his own flight to retrieve her purse.

She hadn't even asked for his help.

Her gaze never wavered as she nervously tapped her foot on the ground, hoping her Good Samaritan would soon reappear. After a few minutes, there was still no sign of Anthony.

"Please, please hurry," she muttered to herself.

"We need to close the cabin door," said the gate agent.

"Just one more minute," she pleaded.

"Everyone's on board. We can't wait any longer."

"That's him!" shouted Olivia.

Still sprinting and weaving, Anthony held the blue and white purse triumphantly above his head. Once her boarding pass and passport were safely in her hands, Olivia and her parents raced down the jet way and boarded the plane. Anthony followed close behind. As they made their way down the aisle, Olivia smiled at Anthony. She then gave him a warm hug while whispering in his ear, "Thank you, thank you, thank you."

After gazing into her eyes one more time, he hurried to his seat in the back of the plane.

During the five-hour flight to New York, Olivia watched a movie, read a book, and thought about the kindness of the stranger who'd rescued her. Once the plane landed, she and her parents disembarked and waited for Anthony. When he finally appeared, Olivia's bubbly mom gave him a hug of her own. "Thanks for being our hero!"

"Happy I could help," he said with a smile.

"Since we had to get on the plane so quickly, we didn't have time to introduce ourselves. My name's Mary Michaels. This is my husband, Andrew. And, of course, you've met Olivia."

"It's nice to meet you all. I'm Anthony."

Olivia drew a deep breath and said, "We're going to get something to eat. Want to join us?"

"Thanks for the offer, but I have a buddy waiting for me at the curb."

"Then give me your number," Olivia boldly replied. "I'll call you when I get back from London. I'd like to take you to lunch to say thanks."

After exchanging numbers, Anthony wished them safe travels. "I hope you have a great time in England," he added.

"Happy New Year, Anthony," said Olivia. "Thanks for being my Good Samaritan!"

He smiled and said, "So glad we both made that flight."

Anthony definitely hoped Olivia would call him after she returned from England. Walking alone, he stopped to admire a Christmas tree in an open area of the terminal. Two soldiers wearing Army uniforms appeared on his right, also looking at the decorated tree.

"Thanks for your service to our country," said Anthony.

"You're welcome, man."

"Where have you been serving?" he asked.

"Afghanistan."

Anthony offered to buy the soldiers something to eat.

"Our flight leaves pretty soon," replied one of the men. "But thanks anyway."

Walking away from the soldiers, Anthony remembered a photo of his own dad looking strikingly handsome in his Army uniform. But there was a look of sadness in his dad's eyes. Serving in Afghanistan, so far from the family he adored, had been a lonely burden for Anthony's dad.

It was also a painful trial for his wife and children back home.

Anthony thought about his dad lying critically wounded on the ground before he died. Fellow soldiers surrounded him, desperately trying to save his life. It devastated Anthony to know that his dad had died more than 8,000 miles from home, without a single family member nearby.

Ten years after his dad's death, Anthony still missed so many things about him. Seeing his dad joke with his mom. Hearing him pray. Looking up and seeing him in the stands at basketball games.

He also missed hearing his dad's favorite saying: *Love is what we've been through together.*

Walking through the sprawling airport, Anthony was surprised by the tears stinging his eyes.

# Chapter 2
## *A Treasure*

Andrew and Mary Michaels held hands as they hurried toward Westminster Abbey in a rain so light it was almost only a mist. Tomorrow they'd be reluctantly returning home, though there was so much more they still wanted to see.

Olivia checked her *London A-Z* book and then craned her neck to see farther down Victoria Street.

"Can you see the spires?" she asked. She was worried the Abbey would close before they could get there.

"Relax," her dad said. "I'm sure we'll see it soon."

A few minutes later, they rounded a tall office building and saw the white spires piercing the London sky.

To Olivia, stepping into Westminster Abbey felt like being carried back in time. The Gothic architecture fascinated her with its pointed arches, ribbed vaulting, and rose windows.

"Was the Abbey bombed during World War II?" Andrew asked a guide.

"The Nazis heavily bombed London, but the Abbey suffered only one direct strike. No one was killed. Part of the roof was destroyed, and many treasures were moved from the Abbey to safer locations. "

As her dad spoke with the guide, Olivia and her mom moved slowly from one grave to the next.

"I never knew so many famous people were buried here," Mary said to Olivia. "Sir Isaac Newton. George Frederic Handel. Charles Dickens. William Wilberforce.*"*

That last name carried the most significance for Mary, as she'd been deeply touched by the movie *Amazing Grace,* which told the story of

Wilberforce's courageous campaign to abolish slavery in the British Empire.

For Olivia, the most poignant moment of their trip took place when she and her parents stood on the docks in Liverpool as a heavy rain pounded their umbrellas. In the 19th century, more than 50,000 British converts to the LDS Church immigrated to the United States. Many departed from Liverpool, including James and Margaret Michaels, Olivia's great-great-great grandfather and great-great-great grandmother.

James and Margaret had set sail with their three young children in 1856, bound for America. Howling winds, fierce waves, and miserable seasickness plagued their voyage, but they finally arrived safely in New York. They then survived the arduous trek to the Salt Lake Valley, while so many other pioneers lost their lives making similar crossings of the sea and plains.

The British Museum, Stonehenge, and Buckingham Palace had also fascinated Olivia. She was inspired by the Florence Nightingale Museum that honored the famous nurse who left a life of privilege to care for those injured in war. Her thoughts soon turned to her Grandma Angela's brave service as an Army nurse in Italy during World War II.

For Olivia, spending time with her parents had been another highlight of the trip. Like all parents, they had their quirks. But she usually found these idiosyncrasies endearing. And she felt grateful to have been raised in a home where she was treated like a treasure.

On the return flight from London to New York, her parents were seated next to each other, while Olivia sat alone farther back in the plane. Eating a nice meal in a comfortable seat, she marveled at the contrast between the way she was crossing the Atlantic and the way her ancestors crossed it. To those 19th century converts, the idea of flying over the ocean at more than 500 miles per hour would've been a miracle as incomprehensible as the parting of the Red Sea.

A married couple behind Olivia began to loudly complain. The wife had expected a better selection of movies. The husband was frustrated that the flight was taking so long.

"It seems like we've been on this plane forever," he griped.

As the plane descended into New York City, Olivia saw the Statue of Liberty in the distance. She imagined her Italian great-grandmother, Gabriela Rossi, seeing that inspiring statue when she arrived in America in 1914 at the age of sixteen.

After a brief layover in New York, Olivia and her parents departed for home. She was able to sit by her parents on this flight, but conversation was scant because both of them soon fell asleep. Her father began to snore thunderously, but Olivia had a proven technique for dealing with this situation. She lightly pinched his nose, which caused him to close his mouth, resettle in his seat, and resume breathing more smoothly.

Olivia's thoughts drifted to her service as a missionary in Rome. When she set foot in that beautiful land, she felt alone in a sea of strangers. The Italians spoke so much faster than her MTC instructors that it made her head spin. Plus, she faced more rejection in her first week than in her entire life up to that point.

Then, something remarkable happened. On a sunny November morning, while riding on a bus past the Colosseum, Olivia struck up a conversation with a friendly Italian girl. Isabella was a 21-year-old college student who'd lived in the United States for a year and spoke excellent English. She happily agreed to meet with Olivia and her companion.

Their first appointment went well. Isabella came to church the following Sunday and told the missionaries she'd already read half of the Book of Mormon.

Six weeks later, Olivia and her companion found themselves filling the font for Isabella's baptism later that evening. Isabella was supposed to arrive for the baptismal service at six o'clock, but surprised Olivia by arriving an hour early. The first thing Isabella said when she saw the missionaries was, "I'm so sorry, but I can't be baptized."

Shocked and disappointed, Olivia was about to ask Isabella why she couldn't be baptized. Then she felt a clear spiritual prompting to pray.

"Isabella, can we kneel and say a prayer together?" she asked in a soft voice.

Olivia knelt and folded her arms. Her companion did the same. After a short pause, Isabella also knelt to join the two missionaries in prayer.

At first, no one spoke. The only sound was the running water filling the baptismal font. Olivia then asked Isabella to offer a prayer. Isabella was hesitant at first. Then, after a long pause, she bowed her head and began to pray.

She thanked God for sending his Son to atone for our sins. She gave thanks for the restoration of the Gospel of Jesus Christ and for the love she felt whenever she was with her two missionaries.

After Isabella finished her prayer, she remained on the floor with her arms folded and head bowed. When she finally spoke, she said, "I want to be baptized tonight."

Isabella's baptism was the pinnacle of a mission filled with many wonderful moments and some very hard trials. Olivia never asked Isabella why she'd initially said she couldn't be baptized that day.

She was baptized in the end, and that was all that mattered. And Isabella's path in the Gospel eventually led her to be sealed in the Swiss Temple to a returned missionary from northern Italy. They were now the proud parents of a baby girl.

After returning to Savona Springs, Olivia went outside and looked up at the stars. Her Grandma Angela often said, "The darker the night, the brighter the stars." Of course, rather than making a statement about astronomy, she was talking about those brave souls who shine in times of difficulty and hardship.

As she lingered under the night sky, Olivia didn't want to think about her former boyfriend, Ty Bradwell. But she struggled to forget his megawatt smile, the adorable dimple in his chin, his deep blue eyes, and the way he callously broke her heart.

# Chapter 3
## *The Good Samaritan*

The next morning, Olivia sent a text to Anthony. *Want to meet me for lunch today?*

Anthony's response came faster than she'd expected. *That'd be great. Where?*

They settled on Michelangelo's Pizza, which was known for its calzones and desserts.

Although Anthony and Olivia had agreed to meet at noon, he was feeling nervous and arrived twenty minutes early. On the basketball court, ice water ran through his veins. But when he was with a pretty girl, his shy side often surfaced.

Anthony took a seat near the front of the restaurant. A young boy recognized him and asked for an autograph. Anthony borrowed a pen from the hostess desk and wrote a personalized message on a napkin for the boy. He then noticed Olivia out of the corner of his eye. Wearing jeans and a casual shirt, she looked completely relaxed in her environment.

Olivia waited for Anthony to finish talking with the autograph seeker, noting how he encouraged the boy to work hard on his grades as well as his basketball skills.

Olivia and Anthony then greeted each other with a warm hug.

"Thanks again for saving my trip," she said, smiling warmly.

He paused for a moment. He'd forgotten how much he liked her smile.

"Anytime. It wasn't that big of a deal. I actually grabbed a bite to eat while I was at Happy Landings. It killed two birds with one stone."

"Ha! So that's why it took you so long to get back. Well, what do you want for lunch today? Should we split a pizza?"

14

"I'd love to," he replied. "Could we make my half just cheese with no pepperoni?"

"I'd rather just have cheese, too."

After they placed their order, she said, "My friend works as a gate agent at the airport. She told me the last week of December is crazy busy. All the flights that week from Savona Springs to New York City were sold out. If I'd missed my flight, I probably never would've made it to London. Thanks to you, I had a great trip."

Olivia then handed him a nicely wrapped box.

He smiled. "What's this? You didn't need to get me anything."

"Oh, it's just an empty box," said Olivia playfully. "I thought you could use it if we have any leftover pizza."

Anthony laughed. "If this box is empty, it's made from the heaviest cardboard on earth. You really didn't need to do this."

"Yes, I did," replied Olivia. "You didn't just save my trip. You put your own trip at risk just to help me."

Inside the box was a painting of the Good Samaritan helping the man who fell among thieves. It was elegantly framed in dark wood.

"Wow," said Anthony. "This means a lot."

"You're welcome. I thought you might like it. You Samaritans have a pretty tightknit group."

"So, tell me about your trip," said Anthony. "How was jolly old England?"

"I loved every minute of it. Stonehenge, Buckingham Palace, Westminster Abbey, the museums, the castles. There's so much to see there."

After a pause, she added, "By the way, my dad thought you looked familiar when we met at the airport. This morning, he realized where he'd seen you. You're on the SSU basketball team. He said you're a super good player."

"I'm a pretty good shooter, but my coach says I'm one of the world's worst passers. So, tell your dad to watch some game film before he praises me too much. And there are plenty of other things I don't do well. Like, I have a really hard time remembering where I put my phone. My roommates are always making fun of me for it."

Olivia laughed. "I feel your pain."

"So, tell me more about yourself," he said.

"I was born here in Savona Springs. I went to BYU for three years before I served a mission in Italy."

"Which mission?"

"Rome."

"My cousin served in Rome," replied Anthony. "Did you know an Elder Kingston from Twin Falls?"

"Yeah, we were in the Napoli district for two transfers. He was a great missionary. But his passing abilities were terrible, so it makes sense you two are related. Speaking of which, other than basketball, what kind of sports do you like?"

"I love to run and hike. It's great living so close to the mountains."

"I run and hike, too," Olivia said. "In high school I was on the cross-country team. I actually came close to making the BYU team."

"That's awesome. The coaches were probably just jealous of your talents and didn't want you showing them up. So, where do you live now?"

"I'm living with my mom and dad, but in a few months, I'm moving into an apartment with one of my friends."

"How is it living with the parents?"

"Oh, it's a dream come true to be 28, single, and living in my parents' basement."

Anthony stared at her awkwardly, hoping he hadn't brought up a sore subject.

"Just kidding," she said with a smile. "I like living at home. My mom and dad are fun and easy to be around."

"What's your favorite movie?" he then asked.

She paused. "I think *The Princess Bride* is my favorite. It's got so many classic lines. And *Chariots of Fire*, since it's about running. You?"

"My favorite movie is *Amazing Grace*," Anthony said. "I admire all that William Wilberforce did to end slavery in the British Empire."

"That's one of my mom's favorite movies," she replied. "It's awesome that we both like old movies!"

"Tell me a bit more about your parents," said Anthony.

"My dad's a physician. He was called to be the bishop of a Young Single Adult ward a couple years ago and I go to his ward. He worries that some of his ward members are too hard on themselves. He actually puts me in that group."

"I can relate to being too hard on myself sometimes," Anthony said. "After every basketball game, I think more about the shots I missed than the shots that I made. Besides loving *Amazing Grace*, what's your mom like?"

"She's lots of fun and a great listener. She spends a lot of her time with her dad. My grandma died two years ago and now he's quite lonely. He just turned 90, and my mom helps him every day."

16

"Good for her," said Anthony. "It's important to be there for family. Now, tell me something you learned in Italy."

"My mission president reminded us that the Savior is the only perfect person to live on this earth. The rest of us are imperfect. He told us that if we can't learn to love imperfect people, we'll live a life without love."

Anthony nodded his head. "I like that. I have a buddy who's a total perfectionist. He's stopped dating lots of great girls because he felt that they had too many flaws. Somehow, he can't see his own flaws. He served a mission in Paris. His girlfriend bought him this beautiful glass globe with the Eiffel Tower inside, but there's a tiny air bubble in the glass. That bubble bothers him so much that he keeps the globe in his closet and only brings it out when his girlfriend comes over. He lets little things annoy him so much."

"That's sad," Olivia said. "I wouldn't want to be around someone who turns little things into such big things."

Olivia then changed the subject, surprising Anthony by asking, "What's your favorite dessert?"

"I love any kind of ice cream. And donuts with chocolate frosting and sliced almonds on top. How about you?"

"The best thing in the world is my Grandma Angela's coconut chocolate chip cookies. They're great. I'll get you some."

"Sign me up," said Anthony. "So, have you found a job here in Savona Springs?"

"Yep. It doesn't pay very well, but I feel I can make a difference there. I'm working for The Melby Foundation. It's a charity set up by Lee Melby and his wife, Ann."

"I know them well," Anthony said. "They're major SSU basketball boosters and their seats are right behind our bench."

"Last year, the Melbys lost a three-year-old granddaughter in a swimming pool accident. They started the foundation to help reduce accidental deaths and injuries involving children."

Anthony shook his head. "That's so sad. I didn't know that happened."

"Children under the age of five are actually more likely to die from drowning than from car accidents," she said. "That's why The Melby Foundation is stressing the need to teach swimming lessons to very young children. We can't eliminate all drowning accidents, but we can hopefully raise awareness."

"How early can you start teaching children to swim?" asked Anthony.

"Some kids learn to swim before they can walk."

Her phone began ringing. "Sorry, I've got to answer this."

Anthony was impressed that Olivia apologized for taking the call. A week earlier, he'd had lunch with a girl who took three long calls during their conversation and didn't seem to think it was a big deal at all.

After quickly finishing her phone call, Olivia turned back to Anthony. "So, do you get your athletic abilities from your parents?" she asked.

"My dad played on the SSU basketball team, but my mom isn't really that athletic. She plays the piano, violin, and harp. And she sings. Sadly, I can't carry a tune in a bucket."

"I'm sure you can sing."

"No, it's awful. Sounds like a sick cow. I just appreciate music from afar."

"I definitely love music, too," she said. "Has your family always lived here in Savona Springs?"

"Nope. I was an Army brat. We lived in Texas and North Carolina, then in Germany for a couple years."

"That doesn't sound too bad. I've heard Germany is incredible. I've always wanted to go there."

"It was actually my second-favorite place to live. I loved the castles. But Savona Springs is the best. We were here for a while and life was just about perfect. Then my dad was sent to Afghanistan. We really felt his absence. He had always been present in our lives…the kind of dad who spends time *with* his kids, not just *around* them."

Anthony was silent for what seemed to Olivia a very long time. He then said, "He hadn't been deployed very long when we received word that he'd been killed in action. That was ten years ago, when I was just 16."

Olivia was stunned. She reached across the table and took Anthony's hand. Tears welled up in her eyes.

"How is your mom doing?" she asked softly.

"For the first year after Dad died, she was pretty much out of commission. She still misses him every day. She cries sometimes, but not as much as before."

"Your dad's death must have been extremely hard for you, too."

"It was terrible. We were really close."

"How did your mom and dad meet?"

"They met at Mamma's Place. It's a restaurant close to campus. It's actually still in business. My mom earned money for college by working there five nights a week."

18

Lost in thought, Anthony pictured in his mind his mom and dad meeting for the first time at that kitschy, little restaurant.

"My mom loved my dad's smile from the first time she saw him," explained Anthony. "And he was a big tipper, even though he was just a poor college student."

"That's a sweet tribute to your dad," she said.

He smiled. "Thanks. I think you're a really kind person, too."

"That's nice to say, but you barely know me."

"I see kindness in your eyes," he said. "I also hear it in your voice."

She looked at him fondly.

"I'd love to take you to Mamma's Place sometime," he said.

"I'd like that a lot."

Long after they'd finished their food, the pair continued talking about movies, books, basketball, hiking, running, and missions. Their conversation was as smooth and natural as the rhythm of the ocean on the seashore.

"Do you want to go with me to the Institute fireside on Sunday?" Olivia asked Anthony as they walk together to her car.

"Jinx," he replied. "I was literally just about to ask you the same thing."

Olivia smiled once more. He saw in that final expression a touch of intrigue, much like the smile of DaVinci's famous *Mona Lisa*. It made him wonder if she might be harboring some type of secret heartache or regret.

Before going to bed that night, Anthony placed the painting of the Good Samaritan on his desk, near a photo of his dad. He then sent a text to Olivia. *Thanks for lunch and thanks for the painting. So thoughtful of you.*

After she received Anthony's message, she opened her Bible to the Gospel of Luke and read about the Good Samaritan. *And he went to him and bound up his wounds, pouring in oil and wine, and set him on his own beast, and brought him to an inn, and took care of him.*

The final four words, *and took care of him*, touched her deeply.

*That's what love is all about,* she thought. *Wives and husbands taking care of each other, their children, and sometimes their parents. Friends taking care of each other. Sometimes even strangers take care of each other, like the kind stranger who risked missing his own flight to help a girl he didn't know.*

*She hadn't even asked for his help.*

# Chapter 4
## *Light*

One of the joys of living at home again was that Olivia's 94-year-old grandma was only a block away. The day after her lunch with Anthony, she went to pay a visit.

Olivia loved visiting her vivacious Grandma Angela for two reasons. First, Angela still had a mind like a steel trap and was one of the wisest people Olivia had ever met. Also, she knew that Angela craved their time together. Her husband had passed away seven years earlier and she missed him dearly.

"Your home smells delicious," said Olivia. "Are you making your famous coconut chocolate chip cookies?"

"Yes, the first batch is in the oven right now. Come join me in the kitchen and tell me all about your trip."

Olivia proceeded to give her grandma a detailed account of their vacation, including her visit to the Florence Nightingale Museum.

"When I served as a nurse in Italy, I often thought about Florence Nightingale," recalled Angela. "She was the real deal."

Angela was silent for a few moments, lost in thought. She then said, "How about some gelato to go with the cookies?"

"I'd love some," Olivia replied with a smile.

As they sat at the kitchen table, the timer sounded and Angela fetched the first batch of cookies from the oven. They smelled heavenly.

Angela then surprised Olivia by saying, "Please close your eyes."

Olivia dutifully closed her eyes.

"Without opening them, tell me five things that are in this kitchen."

"Well, there's a chair, a refrigerator, a table, a toaster, and my beautiful grandma." Olivia then opened her eyes.

"I don't know that 'beautiful' is the best descriptor," Angela said with a laugh. "I'd probably refer to myself as 'weathered.' But all the things you mentioned are in this kitchen. Except you forgot to mention the most important thing."

Olivia was puzzled. "What's that?"

"*Light.* This room is full of light. Take away the light and we couldn't see anything. When we walk in the light, we see other people in the same light that our Father in Heaven sees them. We see every person as a son or daughter of God. We see every person as our spiritual brother or sister."

"I've never thought about it like that."

Angela smiled. "I love light. To me, it's a miracle."

After a brief pause, Angela asked, "So, do you have any good dating prospects these days?"

"I might. On the day we flew to England, I was totally distracted and forgot my purse at a restaurant. I was about to miss my flight when a stranger offered to run and get it. He was really fast, but still only got back with a few seconds to spare."

"How nice that a stranger helped you."

"What touched me most was that he was on the same flight that I was on. When he took off running to get my purse, he was putting his own flight at risk. And I never even asked him to do that. He just volunteered."

Angela smiled. "It's always nice to have a Good Samaritan around when you need one."

"Yes, it is. I've never been to an SSU basketball game, but I know you go to most of them. My Good Samaritan was Anthony Hull."

"Really? He's one of my favorite players."

"I actually had lunch with him right before I came here. He's cute and nice and a little shy."

"Your mom told me that you dated a law school student for a long time," said Angela. "It seemed like things were going well, then all of a sudden he stopped dating you."

"His name is Ty," Olivia said softly. "I met him about a year ago at a Christmas party in Provo. Ty was one of the last to arrive and he totally owned the room. Almost every girl, including me, stopped to admire him.

"Later that evening, Ty introduced himself. He was really charismatic and confident. He told me that he was a 3L and would graduate near the end of April. I told him that I'd be graduating the following December with my Masters.

"I was actually surprised when he asked me out that night. I thought he was out of my league. He seemed a bit arrogant, but there was a lot to like about him. Soon we were dating exclusively. I felt better about myself when I was with him. He was nice and never criticized me. The last thing I want is a husband who would judge me. I'm already hard enough on myself. With each passing month, I fell more deeply in love.

"After seven years in Provo, he wanted to live in a city with mild winters. I encouraged him to interview with some law firms here in Savona Springs. It didn't take long. He received a job offer from a great firm.

"One night in June, he took me to a nice restaurant. We'd been dating about six months. I thought he was about to propose, but he didn't. I was disappointed, but I still thought he'd propose to me before he left town. He was going to move to Savona Springs in mid-July.

"We went to the Stadium of Fire in Provo. Ty seemed distant. The next day, I called him to see if he wanted to go on a hike. He didn't answer, so I sent him a text. He still didn't respond.

"I went to his apartment the next morning to make sure he was alright. I thought he might be sick or something. His roommate invited me in. I asked him if Ty was there. He said that Ty had left the day before. He'd decided to move right away because his apartment in Savona Springs became available sooner than expected. His roommate was shocked that Ty had left without even telling me goodbye. So was I."

Olivia and Angela were both silent. Finally, Olivia said, "I felt like I'd given so much to our relationship. I really tried to make him happy. But he vanished like a thief in the night. When I got back to my apartment, I was glad none of my roommates were there. I just curled up on my bed for a few hours."

Angela had tears in her eyes. She gently took Olivia by the hand and said, "I'm so sorry."

After a long pause, Angela asked, "What made you fall in love with Ty?"

"He was kind and never criticized me. He was nice to everyone. One of my friends was in his ward and Ty was her home teacher. She said that he came every month and always asked how he could help her. When she moved out at the end of spring semester, Ty was the only person there to help."

"Your grandpa never criticized me," said Angela. "And he was quick to give compliments. That's one of the reasons I miss him so much. You don't get many compliments when you live alone. The only benefit is you win more arguments, I guess."

22

"I have a compliment for you," Olivia said, taking hold of her grandma's hand. "You're my hero."

Once again, Angela's eyes filled with tears. "Thank you, but I don't feel like much of a hero. Just an old woman who cares about her granddaughter. So please tell me more about this strange, disappearing boyfriend of yours."

"After Ty left, I was devastated," Olivia said. "My confidence was shattered, and I felt this overwhelming feeling of sadness."

"That's perfectly normal," Angela replied. "Sometimes, we have to feel bad before we feel good. It's part of the grieving process. And that process takes time."

"After about a week, I decided that I didn't want to be like Lot's wife. I refused to look back. I was going to keep moving forward, pour some concrete down my spine, and forget about Ty Bradwell."

Angela smiled. "I'm glad you picked yourself up and got on with your life. Did you really never hear from him again?"

"A little while after Ty vanished, I received a text. I've read it so many times that I probably have it memorized. He said he was sorry he didn't talk to me in person before leaving Provo. He loved dating me. He said I was the kindest person he had ever dated, but he thought we should both move on. Then he told me he knew I'd make a wonderful wife for someone and would be a great mom."

Angela shook her head. "You dated Ty for seven months, and instead of saying goodbye in person, he sends you a text one week later? He may be gorgeous, but it seems to me that he's also a self-centered dud who didn't have the courage to talk to you face-to-face."

"Don't get too upset, Grandma. It's been six months and I feel much better about it now. I almost never think about him anymore."

"I remember you running a race at Veteran's Park when you were in high school," Angela said. "A runner accidently tripped you. You fell and cut your knee. Blood was running down your leg, but you started running even faster. You actually passed three other runners after you tripped and fell."

"Yeah, I remember that race. I almost passed out."

"Sweetheart, you are one tough cookie. You can handle cutting your knee and you can handle being rejected by a coward. Ty didn't deserve you. You deserve better. A lot better."

"I know. I thought I knew him well, but obviously I didn't."

Angela looked into Olivia's eyes and said, "In my 94 years on this planet, I've learned a lot. There are two things I want to share with you.

The first is that we can never fully understand all of the thoughts and feelings in another person's heart."

"And what's the second?"

"Sometimes we don't fully understand ourselves."

"Ty deeply hurt me," Olivia said. "He left me feeling vulnerable. Like a bird with broken wings."

"Please don't let your experience with Ty hurt your self-confidence. No guy can make you feel inferior unless you give him permission."

"Don't worry, Grandma. To me, Ty is nothing more than a distant memory."

"May I give you another word of advice?"

"Of course," Olivia said.

"Marry someone who is kind. Kindness is the foundation of any happy marriage. Ty does not sound like a kind person to me."

Later that evening, right before going to sleep, Olivia's thoughts returned to Ty. When she'd told her Grandma Angela that he was nothing more than a distant memory, she wasn't completely honest. Ty was hard to forget. She still wondered where their relationship went wrong and if she could've done things differently. Most of all, she yearned for closure.

That night, Angela had a disturbing dream about World War II. She'd had the dream many times before. In it, a young soldier dies despite the valiant efforts of Angela and the other nurses who cared for him night and day. He was good and innocent. But, in a short time, his loved ones would learn that he was gone from this earth.

Angela didn't know anything about the young soldier except that he was a brave young man who had died serving his country. In her dream, she sobbed while reverently placing a white sheet over his face.

Yet another young soldier had died.

Before he married.

Before he had children.

Before he was reunited with his family back home.

This wasn't just a dream. It had happened countless times during Angela's service during the war. She had felt like her heart was breaking every time she covered the face of another soldier.

# Chapter 5
## *The Boss*

When Fletcher Parks walked into a room, the energy level immediately rose. He was equal parts fast walker and fast talker, bristling with enthusiasm for his work. His colleagues called him "The Boss."

Fletcher had graduated from the BYU Law School, served his time at the largest law firm in Savona Springs, then finally ventured off to start the Law Offices of Parks & Lane.

All the attorneys who worked for Fletcher respected him. He was ethical and wise, plus he worked harder than just about anyone else. If he had a vice, it was the occasional moments he'd lose his temper and erupt like a volcano. These usually occurred when one of his attorneys did something he felt was inappropriate. Though rare, his eruptions were always memorable.

When a talented young attorney at the firm received a ticket for driving under the influence of alcohol, the entire office heard Fletcher yelling at him. Fletcher warned him that he'd be fired if he received another DUI. The attorney desperately promised it would never happen again.

To his credit, the young attorney had kept his promise. He knew Fletcher was a man who took promises seriously.

As a young man, Fletcher served an LDS mission in Honduras. He was now married and had three children. He'd been called to serve as a bishop of a Young Single Adult ward in Savona Springs, which was a challenging but rewarding responsibility. He felt that he learned as much from the members of his ward as they learned from him. Maybe even more.

Sitting in his small office at Parks & Lane, Ty Bradwell wanted to scream. One of the senior partners had just informed him that his current supervising partner, whom he considered a mentor and friend, was leaving the firm to become a judge.

Ty's heart sunk even further when told that his new supervising partner would be Rex Lambert. All the young attorneys in the firm knew that Rex was impatient, critical, and demanding. He was about as much fun as a kidney stone. Some of the attorneys even referred to him as "T-Rex."

Ty put his head in his hands and shuddered.

Even under his first supervisor, Ty felt that his job at the firm was overly stressful. He frequently had to work longer hours than he wanted. Looking out the window of his office, there wasn't a cloud in the sky. He began to daydream about playing a round of golf that morning and then spending the afternoon hiking, but he knew that wasn't an option.

Ty stared out the window for a long time before forcing himself to resume work.

# Chapter 6
## *The Bridge*

Anthony called Olivia on Sunday afternoon. "I thought it might be nice if we invited your Grandma Angela to come with us to the fireside tonight. Think she'd want to join us?"

"I'm sure she would," said Olivia.

As the three of them drove to the Institute building, Angela asked Anthony, "What's the key to your success as a basketball player?"

"I've got amazing coaches and teammates."

"That's an awfully humble answer," Angela said.

Anthony paused for a moment. "Well, my high school coach always told us that playing basketball is 90% half-mental."

Angela and Olivia both laughed.

*They're an easy audience*, Anthony thought.

Sister Kathleen Garson, a popular Institute teacher, was the first speaker that evening.

"I've spoken with many young adults, and also many older adults, who feel their life has to be perfect, or almost perfect, before they can be truly happy," she began. "Please don't fall into that trap. In this mortal life, perfection is an impossible goal. If you think, 'I'll be happy once my life is perfect,' you're not going to be happy *or* perfect. We should diligently strive to become more like the Savior, but He is the only perfect person to ever walk on this earth.

"Learn to embrace people who are good, but not perfect. Appreciating the good in others is especially important in marriage. When an imperfect husband and an imperfect wife show each other kindness and understanding, their love always grows.

"It's been said that love is blind, but marriage is a real eye-opener. All newlyweds face surprises and bumps on the road as they try to understand each other better.

"It recently dawned on me that I'd never specifically prayed to love my husband in a more Christ-like way. I knelt in prayer and said, 'Dear Father in Heaven, I feel that I already love my husband with all my heart, but I know that I'm by no means perfect, so please help me to love him even more completely.'

As soon as I finished that prayer, a remarkable wave of love and gratitude came over me. For those of you who are married, I encourage you to pray to love your spouse even more. It will help open your eyes and expand your heart."

Sister Garson closed her talk by sharing an enlightening observation. "We live in a culture that worships outward beauty. It's always nice to take care of our appearance, but remember that inner goodness and outer beauty are not the same things. If we aren't careful, we can start admiring people only because they're beautiful on the outside.

"Instead, we should admire people who are kind and generous. When it comes to dating and marriage, physical attraction is definitely important. But virtues like a loving heart, understanding, and thoughtfulness can add a lot of fuel to the romantic fire. True and lasting beauty is more than skin deep."

"I also encourage you to pray to have a greater love for your family members and friends. Love is the bridge that brings us together."

Ty was also at the fireside that night. His date was a gregarious girl he'd met through a mutual friend. He noticed Olivia sitting a few rows in front of him and was happy to see her smiling and holding hands with Anthony. He'd heard that Anthony was a quality guy.

It had been six months since Ty had last seen Olivia. He still loved and admired her more than any other girl he'd ever dated but had still decided they weren't quite right for each other. In some ways, he actually hoped Olivia would come talk to him. But she didn't notice him.

On the drive home, Angela said to Anthony, "Olivia told me yesterday about some of your father's experiences in the military. He must have been an amazing man. Tomorrow night we're having a special Family Home Evening at my house. I'm going to talk about my time as an Army nurse in Italy during World War II. You're welcome to join us."

"Thanks," Anthony replied. "I'd love to come."

As they pulled into Angela's driveway, she said, "Can you please come inside and sit with me for a minute? I have something for both of you."

She soon returned to the living room with two plates piled high with her scrumptious coconut chocolate chip cookies.

Anthony took a bite. "Okay, these are amazing."

He then noticed an Arnold Freiberg painting on Angela's wall.

"I like Freiberg's paintings, but his depictions of huge men with bulging biceps don't seem very accurate. I work out four days a week and don't look anything like those bodybuilding prophets in his paintings. Maybe the Nephites just had a better workout routine than me."

Grandma Angela laughed and said, "You definitely need some heavier weights. Nephi could teach you a thing or two."

Anthony smiled. "Thanks so much for the advice."

Olivia and Anthony held hands while walking to Olivia's front door. To his very pleasant surprise, she even gave him a goodnight kiss. He then invited her to go on a hike with him on Saturday morning and she gladly accepted.

Her parents were still gone, so Olivia sat alone at the kitchen table, thinking about Anthony as she ate one of Grandma Angela's heavenly cookies. Deep in thought, she continued this process until only a few crumbs remained on the plate. This wasn't the first time she had no memory of eating something because she'd been so preoccupied with other matters. In this case, Olivia was realizing how much she was falling in love with Anthony Hull.

Driving home that night, Anthony also was flying high. Looking back, he was glad he'd rescued Olivia's purse and passport that day when she'd come so close to missing her flight. If not for that decision, she wouldn't have come into his life, as beautiful and unexpected as a shooting star.

# Chapter 7
## *The Lamb and the Lion*

Olivia offered the opening prayer for the Family Home Evening at her Grandma Angela's house. Olivia's parents were there, along with her older brother Jonah, her sister-in-law Robin, and Anthony. Grandpa Ezra Harris, Olivia's maternal grandfather, had planned to come but ended up not feeling well enough to join them.

After the prayer, Olivia's dad said, "Mom, thanks so much for agreeing to share some of your experiences. I know you're sometimes reluctant to talk about your wartime experiences. We get that. Your memories are still very painful, even after more than 70 years. We love you and admire your service to our country. You're an amazing example and a hero in our eyes."

"Thank you, Andrew, for your kind words," said Angela. "Like most veterans, I have talked very little about my service in World War II. But I feel the time has come to share my story with you. I've written up these experiences and will be mailing it to all the family members who aren't able to be here with us tonight.

"My goal is to honor those millions of American men and women who risked their lives to protect our liberties. More than 400,000 Americans made the ultimate sacrifice. Many more suffered devastating injuries. In so many cases, those injuries lasted the rest of their lives. Every person who served our nation in World War II, or any other war, deserves our deepest gratitude. And they deserve to be remembered.

"Although the loss of American lives in World War II was heartbreaking, other countries lost far more. It's estimated that Russia suffered eight million military deaths, Germany lost five million soldiers, and Japan lost two million soldiers. Those numbers don't include the millions of civilians who also died."

Grandma Angela paused for a moment. In a voice filled with emotion, she said, "While I was serving in Anzio, I saw things that no human being should ever have to see. They still haunt me. I often felt that I was trapped inside a nightmare. Tonight, I will talk about death and suffering, but I will not be sharing with you the most disturbing events I witnessed while serving as an Army nurse. I love you too much to put the worst of my memories into your hearts and minds. I wish I could remove them from my own."

*Anzio: A Nurse's Story*

*During World War II, more than 350,000 women, including almost 60,000 registered nurses, volunteered to serve our country. I was one of those nurses.*

*On January 28, 1944, I landed on the beach at Anzio, 35 miles south of Rome. The moment my feet touched Italian soil, I thought of my mom. She was born in Rome. I also thought of that day in 1915 when my mom first came to America as a 16-year-old girl. I took comfort in knowing that my mom, my dad, and my sister Maria were praying for me every single day I was in Italy.*

*I was part of a large group of nurses assigned to "Operation Shingle," a major campaign by the Americans and British to liberate Rome and other areas in Italy from the Nazis.*

*I want to begin with a true story that illustrates Hitler's viciousness. In early 1944, when Nazi soldiers still occupied Rome, a resistance group ambushed and killed 33 German soldiers.*

*Hitler decided on a ruthless response. Not satisfied with "an eye for an eye," he ordered his commander in Rome to kill ten Italians for each German who died in the ambush. Within 24 hours, the Nazis captured and killed 330 Italians. Few, if any, of the murdered Italians had any connection to the ambush of the German soldiers.*

*This story of revenge times ten will help you understand why Operation Shingle was a critically important campaign. Every soldier, doctor, and nurse knew that losing to Hitler and his war machine was not an option.*

*Soon after I arrived at Anzio, a new hospital area was established on a half-acre of flat, sandy beach. The stress of caring for wounded soldiers was something that U.S Army doctors and nurses experienced everywhere, but we faced an additional peril in Anzio. Military field hospitals were normally positioned some distance from the battlefield, but in Anzio, our tents were dangerously close to the combat zone.*

*Leaders had expected our troops to push back the German Army far enough to create a reasonably safe distance between the combat zone and our hospital compound, but it didn't work out that way. Our forces found themselves locked in a stalemate that quickly became a bloodbath.*

Since our hospital tents were already positioned on the beach, if we'd moved any farther away from the battle zone, we would have been floating in the Mediterranean Ocean. We were left out in the open, where enemy soldiers could observe our every move. We were always within the reach of German artillery and they often purposely shelled our hospital tents. One night, the shelling killed five patients and wounded 15 others, including two nurses and a doctor. During the attacks, we would sit in our tents, holding our knees and shaking like leaves in the wind.

We soon learned that if we congregated in groups, like when we went to church together, Nazi forces would fire shells at us, even though it was obvious that we were doctors and nurses. I felt even more frightened when I learned that our Anzio hospital compound was nicknamed, "Hell's Half Acre." After the war, I was told that no other U.S. hospital site in the world endured more enemy attacks than Hell's Half Acre. Some soldiers on the front lines even refused to come to the Anzio hospital tents for treatment when they were injured. They felt safer remaining in the battlefield.

Our food supply often ran short. I wasn't starving, but I usually felt hungry. I love milk and I craved it, but I never once had a glass of milk during my five months in Anzio.

Because the fighting around Anzio was so fierce, we received a steady influx of wounded soldiers, many of them in critical condition. One of our most agonizing challenges was deciding the order in which wounded soldiers would be treated. Sometimes wounded soldiers had to wait for many hours before it was their turn to be placed on the operating room table.

Our shifts lasted 12 hours, but we worked even longer when the numbers of wounded were especially high. I remember one night I worked for 16 hours, went back to my tent and slept for four hours, and then returned to work another 12 hours. My mental and physical fatigue was almost unbearable.

I always felt an overwhelming sadness when wounded soldiers arrived for treatment. They looked afraid and exhausted. Many arrived with shattered limbs or intestines protruding out of their bodies. Soldiers who had been shot in their lungs frantically gasped for air. Since it was often cold and rainy, many soldiers arrived soaked to the bone and shivering after lying in the mud for hours or even days.

Sometimes soldiers whose wounds were not life-threatening would graciously say, "Nurse, don't worry about me. Take care of someone who is worse off." I was deeply touched every time a humble, injured soldier put someone else ahead of him. Those acts of kindness reminded me of something my mother used to say: "The darker the night, the brighter the stars."

In the hospital tents in Anzio, I saw many stars shine brightly.

I felt honored to be a small part of a medical team that saved thousands of lives during the time I served in Anzio. But I shed many tears over those patients we weren't able to save. We weren't perfect doctors and nurses, but we were trying to make a meaningful contribution. My wartime service convinced me that our Father in Heaven wants us to live a life full of meaning and purpose, not a life overly focused on superficial pursuits. He wants us to make a difference. When I was helping a suffering soldier, I felt that I was using my time on this earth in a way that mattered.

I spent much of my time assisting during surgery. I also did other tasks, such as administering blood and plasma, cleaning and bandaging wounds, supplying penicillin to those with infections, and giving morphine shots to relieve severe pain. Those soldiers would beg, or even scream, for morphine.

I'm haunted by the times I heard severely wounded soldiers cry out for their mothers to help them. It happened over and over again. It reminded me that the bond between mother and child is strong and sacred.

There was one patient who had fractured both his arms and both legs. He was in a plaster cast from his neck to his feet. Day after day and night after night, he would cry, "Help me, mom." I can still hear the desperate, pleading tone of his voice.

I learned to never, never, never give up on any patient. I vividly remember one soldier who had suffered multiple life-threatening injuries. I was nearly positive he would not survive, but we kept doing everything we could. It was a long and difficult road, but he survived. We actually kept in touch after the war. He married and had four children. He died at the age of 89.

I thanked all the soldiers for their service to our country. Countless times, wounded soldiers thanked me for taking care of them. One soldier proposed to me after I had cared for him for two weeks. I told him that I was already engaged. That was a fib, but I didn't have the heart to just reject him.

One of my saddest days as a nurse was February 7, 1944, just 10 days after I arrived in Anzio. That day, a British pilot was in hot pursuit of a German plane. To escape, the German pilot decided to increase his speed by reducing his weight. He released all the bombs that he was carrying. The bombs were jettisoned directly over our hospital compound. They landed, one after another, on our tents.

I had finished my shift an hour before those bombs struck, so I raced back to help. It was truly a horrific sight. Some tents had been completely destroyed. Others were on fire. I soon came across an injured soldier covered by debris.

"I'm going to die!" he cried over and over again. He died as I tried to free him.

I watched two other soldiers die on the operating table that day, but our medical teams also saved many lives in the aftermath of the bombs. After my long hours of work were over, I started walking back to my tent. I came across a row of cots, on which lay the bodies of many of those who had been killed. The face and the body of each victim was covered by a blanket, but the blankets were too short to cover their feet.

When I saw nurses' shoes on two of the dead bodies, I began to sob uncontrollably. More than 70 years after that dreadful day, I still vividly remember seeing the shoes of my fellow nurses sticking out from under those blankets.

Those bombs killed 28 people, including three nurses, one Red Cross worker, two officers, and 22 enlisted men. Just a few days later, tragedy struck again. Two more nurses were killed when a large shell fired by German troops hit the tent in which they slept. On that same day, another attack left one of our Army nurses with a severe chest wound. She died several days later. Her name was Mary and she was one of my closest friends.

I started having severe panic attacks. I had trouble falling asleep. After I fell asleep, the nightmares took hold.

During my first few months in Anzio, we often had to deal with heavy rainstorms that created fields of deep mud. The bodies of many dead soldiers were never recovered from those muddy fields. It is terrible to bury a loved one, but it is even more terrible to never find any remains of a loved one to bury.

Our hospital tents housed a mixture of putrid smells I will never forget, including lots of blood and lots of sweat. Some soldiers returned home blind or deaf or severely depressed. Others had complete psychiatric breakdowns. Seeing all the various types of physical, emotional, and mental suffering inflicted by war, I came to fully understand those three simple words: "War is Hell."

In spite of hell-like conditions, I witnessed many acts of courage and love. One newly arrived nurse lost her helmet when it fell from a boat into the ocean right before she landed. A veteran nurse kindly gave her own helmet to the new nurse, even though having no helmet increased the risk of death. It was several days before a replacement helmet arrived for that unselfish veteran nurse.

I remember two brothers serving together in Anzio. The younger brother had been wounded, so his older brother came to visit him in his hospital tent. During the visit, a bomb directly struck the tent. The older brother had heard the incoming bomb, so he threw himself like a blanket over his younger brother. The older brother was hit in the head, neck, and back by shrapnel. He died instantly. The younger brother was saved thanks to his brother's quick and heroic actions. I have never forgotten that Christ-like act of brotherly love.

When I wasn't performing my nursing duties, my mind often turned to thoughts of home. Words cannot describe how much I longed to be with my family. They wrote me often, but many of the letters never arrived.

Nazi soldiers once shelled the hospital tent where I worked. I was on duty, but fortunately I was not injured. Many others were not as fortunate. Five patients were killed and 18 were wounded, some very seriously.

I felt so vulnerable. So exposed. I told my tentmate, "I wish I had more courage. I'm only 21 and I don't want to die. Where do you get your courage?"

She was a very experienced 34-year-old nurse. She gave me a new and enlightened vision when she said, "Courage isn't the absence of fear. Courage is doing the right thing in spite of your fears. You always do your duty, Angela. That shows me that you are courageous."

Her caring comments gave me the comfort I badly needed.

34

One of the happiest days of my life was June 5, 1944. The Nazis had been driven back and Rome was finally liberated. As I walked with my fellow nurses through the streets of Rome, we were showered with flowers, cheers, and warm hugs by the celebrating throngs.

The Romans became even more excited when I began to speak with them in the fluent Italian I learned from my mom, who was born and raised in Rome before moving to the United States.

I was stunned by the beauty and history of Rome but cringed when I saw the Colosseum. After witnessing the brutality of war, I couldn't imagine how the ancient Romans found pleasure in seeing gladiators fight to the death. I also thought about the apostles Peter and Paul as I walked through the city where they preached and ultimately gave their lives because of their firm commitment to Christ.

The next day, as we drove back to Anzio, our jeep overturned and my leg was very badly broken. The pain of the break was almost unbearable. One week later, I was on a ship bound for the United States. By the time my leg had healed, the war was over.

I would like to conclude by sharing with you the most sacred experience that I had during my service. After the war, I shared this experience only with my husband, but I now want my posterity to know about it as well.

It happened late at night on May 11, 1944. My tentmate had gone on a walk with a friend, so I was alone. I knelt down and poured out my heart, asking God for comfort, peace, and protection. At the end of my prayer, I felt prompted to sing "The Spirit of God." It was a hymn I loved, and I knew every verse by heart.

Alone in my tent, still on my knees, I sang the first verse quietly. The second verse I sang with more emotion. By the third verse, I was belting out the words loud enough for others to hear.

And then, late at night in war-torn Italy, I began to sing the final verse of the hymn. It tells of the triumphant return of the Prince of Peace, when war will cease, and this world will again become a true paradise. As I sang, something changed within me. Surrounded by the darkness of war, I finished the hymn's final verse with a perfect brightness of hope.

How blessed the day when the lamb and the lion
Shall lie down together without any ire,
And Ephraim be crowned with his blessing in Zion
As Jesus descends with his chariot of fire!
We'll sing and we'll shout with the armies of heaven,
Hosanna, hosanna to God and the Lamb!
Let glory to them in the highest be given,
Henceforth and forever, Amen and amen!

*As I finished singing that sacred hymn, a wave of warmth swept through my body, starting at the top of my head and ending with my feet. I felt our Heavenly Father's divine love more profoundly than ever before. From that day on, I was a different person. I still experienced fear and anxiety, but I felt much more at peace. I knew that God was aware of me and that He loved me.*

*I consider each day of my life since the war a sacred gift. I will never forget the moment I was reunited with the family that I loved so much. But my joy was tinged with great sorrow for all those not as fortunate. So very, very many returned with horrific injuries. Or never returned at all.*

*As the daughter of an Italian mother and an American father, and as a former U.S Army nurse who cared for the wounded and the dying on Italian soil, I rejoice that there is now a holy temple in Rome.*

*To me, it is a breathtaking miracle that Latter-day Saints in Italy have a sacred place of divine peace in that beautiful land. Where my mother was born and where the apostles Peter and Paul preached of Christ and gave their lives in His service. Finally, the Eternal City has a truly eternal temple.*

*I know that my Redeemer lives. I do not know when Christ's Second Coming will occur, but each day brings us closer to that promised time when there will be no more wars and the lamb and the lion will peacefully lie down together.*

*I say these things, and I express my love to each of you, in the name of Jesus Christ,* amen.

# Chapter 8
## *Lost and Found*

On a gorgeous Saturday morning, light streamed into Olivia's pink and white bedroom. She liked being back in the bedroom she'd shared with her sister when they were younger. It seemed much smaller to her now. She realized, of course, that the size of the room hadn't changed. Her perspective had.

She was planning to go on a hike with Anthony at noon. Just a few minutes after she woke up, he called and told her that a five-year-old girl named Lily had wandered away from a campsite the prior evening in Kimball Canyon, just outside of Savona Springs. The girl was still missing, so more volunteers were needed to help search for her.

Olivia told Anthony that she could be ready in five minutes.

When they arrived at the search center, they were asked to explore a rugged area north of the canyon road. More than two hundred volunteers were already searching for the young girl, with additional volunteers expected to arrive soon.

"I can't imagine the fear that Lily's parents are feeling right now," Olivia said.

"They must be terrified," replied Anthony. "She's only five and she had to spend the night outdoors and alone."

Thirty minutes later, they watched a wonderful scene unfold. The worried mother finally caught sight of her lost girl. One of the volunteers had found the child lying beneath a tree and was carrying her back down the road. The mother raced toward them, joyously yelling, "Lily! Lily! Lily!"

When she reached her daughter, the mother fell to her knees and cradled her like an infant. Lily's dad soon sprinted over to join them.

A precious child who had been lost was now found.

Olivia looked at Anthony and noticed tears in his eyes.

After the harrowing search for Lily, Anthony and Olivia felt a burst of energy. They decided to hike to a lake that was five miles away. They moved at a fast pace and soon found themselves walking single file on a narrow trail.

"Be careful," said Olivia. "It's a long way down. Are you afraid of heights?"

"Nope," Anthony said with a smile. "But I'm afraid of widths."

She laughed and shook her head.

After they'd walked a bit further, Olivia suggested they take a brief break. She reached into her backpack and handed Anthony a donut with chocolate frosting and sliced almonds on top.

"Wow!" he exclaimed. "I'm impressed you remembered that I love these donuts. Let's split it."

"That's nice of you to offer, but I have two donuts. One for each of us."

When they reached the lake, they sat on a smooth rock, basking in the beauty and stillness of nature. Gazing at her, Anthony felt a rush of affection. He wanted to say something poetic and creative, but he wasn't quite sure what that might be, so he just smiled at her. Finally, he said, "Tell me something surprising that happened while you were in Italy."

She paused. "Right after I arrived in southern Italy, I lost my nametag while riding on a bus."

"I wouldn't necessarily call that surprising," Anthony joked. "You're kind of an expert at misplacing things."

"Don't interrupt," she said with a grin. "I haven't gotten to the good part yet. Anyhow, I got down on my hands and knees to look for my nametag, and an old man started helping me. Soon, at least seven or eight other passengers were crawling around looking for it. That's one thing I love most about Italians—they're so willing and anxious to help. A few moments later, the old man found my nametag."

"I love that," he said. "Sometimes it can be hard to know how to help people, so I always appreciate it when strangers just jump in. One time at Disney World, my family was standing in line behind a little girl and her parents. She was wearing mouse ears. She looked so happy.

Anthony paused. "I'm not sure why, but the little girl's parents started to argue. They got louder and angrier. And that poor girl looked terrified. She started to cry. Then her mom yelled that she was leaving and stormed out of the park. The girl stood there by her dad, sobbing.

"That was ten or eleven years ago, but I remember the heartbroken look on that girl's face. I wanted so badly to help, but I just didn't know what I could do to make things better for her. I felt so powerless. And I still sometimes wonder how things turned out for that girl."

"That's just too sad," Olivia said softly. "It hurts my heart when kids have to go through things like that."

She then pointed to the sky. "Does that cloud look like a sailboat to you?"

He nodded. "It really does. Imagine if clouds only appeared one day a year. Families would probably go to the park and lay down on a blanket to enjoy the annual cloud show, just like they do for Fourth of July fireworks. We see clouds all the time, so we take them for granted. My dad always said that taking things for granted is the opposite of being grateful."

"What else do you think we take for granted?" she asked.

"Our freedom. The blessings of the Gospel. Our health. Having plenty to eat. Sometimes we even take the people we love most for granted."

"You're right," she said.

"I'll never forget the day that I learned my dad had been killed. My mom asked me to go the store to get a few things. She was too devastated to leave the house. It was like any other day at the store. People were smiling and kids were laughing. My world had been shattered, but their world hadn't missed a beat. Losing a loved one is such a private ordeal."

She looked into his eyes, took both of his hands gently in hers, and said, "I'm so sorry you lost your dad."

After a long pause, he said, "One thing that helped me after Dad died was remembering that life on this earth is just a small sliver of time from an eternal perspective. I'm sure he misses us, just like we miss him, but I'm also sure that he's learning and growing and having remarkable experiences in the next world."

"I already told you that I have an older brother and a younger brother," Olivia said. "I also have an identical twin sister named Bella, who died just over three years ago."

Anthony was surprised to hear this. "I'm so sorry," he said.

"Most people didn't think we were identical twins. My hair was brown, but Bella bleached her hair blond and wore it longer than mine. She was a teacher at Central Junior High. One day, she was on a bus that was taking the school's orchestra to a competition. A truck driver had a heart attack and crashed into the bus. The front of the bus burst into flames, so no one could exit through the front door. Bella opened a window near the back and helped kids get out, one by one.

"Then she started searching for other kids who might still be on board. Knowing her, she wouldn't leave a single student behind. While she was making a final search of the bus, she passed out from inhaling so much smoke.

"The firefighters found her on the floor of the bus. She was still alive, but she died in the ambulance on her way to the hospital. All the students Bella helped get out of the bus came to her funeral. They gave the most beautiful tributes."

"She sounds like a wonderful and courageous woman," said Anthony.

"Wonderful and courageous are two perfect words to describe Bella. We all have unanswered questions. I wonder why I'm here and Bella is gone. I wonder why my Grandma Angela was married for 62 years, but her identical twin, Maria, never married."

"Did Maria ever come close to getting married?"

"She wanted to, but it never worked out. She was a wonderful nurse and just a happy, loving person. I never knew anyone who had more friends than her. She was actually like a second grandma to me."

Olivia looked skyward and saw an eagle soaring past them on its way over the ridge.

"I love eagles," she said. "When I arrived in the mission field, I was asked to select a scripture to share with the other missionaries. I chose Isaiah 40:31."

She then recited it from memory. *But they that wait upon the Lord shall renew their strength; they shall mount up with wings as eagles; they shall run and not be weary; and they shall walk, and not faint.*

He gently took hold of her hand.

"Look how beautiful," she said, pointing to a rainbow that had appeared on the other side of the lake. She then began to sing one of her favorite songs, an old Lutheran hymn:

*Fair is the sunshine,*
*Fairer the moonlight*
*And all the stars in heav'n above;*
*Jesus shines brighter,*
*Jesus shines purer*
*And brings to all the world his love.*
*Beautiful Savior.*
*Lord of the nations.*
*Son of God and Son of Man.*

*Thee will I honor,*
*Praise, and give glory,*
*Give praise and glory evermore.*

"I could listen to you sing all day," said Anthony. "You really have a gift."

The two of them lingered by the lake for another hour or so. The breeze provided an ideal temperature, and Olivia felt happy and calm. As she gazed at Anthony, she felt she was looking into his heart. She saw kindness and compassion, as well as a certain humility she found endearing.

When she had dated Ty in Provo, she was often drawn to his strong and confident personality. But, at times, his confidence was too much of a good thing. His strength could also be one of his greatest weaknesses.

Sitting together by the peaceful lake, Anthony wanted to tell her that he loved her. Yet, he wondered if it might be too soon.

Olivia then shocked him by looking directly into his eyes and saying, "I love you, Anthony."

He smiled and said, "I love you, too."

After a kiss, they began making their way back down the trail. They were silent for long stretches of the hike, but it was a comfortable silence. Less than a mile from the car, it began to rain. Olivia looked up at the sky so the rain could fall on her face.

*She is so much fun and so easy to love,* thought Anthony.

As Olivia lay in bed that night, she felt at peace. After her awful experience with Ty, it was as though she had locked her broken heart inside a tomb. Thanks to Anthony, her heart felt free again. She was happier than she'd ever been.

# Chapter 9
## *In a Matter of Seconds*

As the setting sun illuminated the spires of the Salt Lake Temple, Olivia pondered a question posed by the Apostle Paul two millennia ago: *Know ye not that ye are the temple of God?*

Earlier that morning, she'd flown to Salt Lake City to witness her cousin's marriage. Her parents very much wanted to come, but they both had the flu and didn't want to pass on their sickness as a wedding gift to the newlyweds.

During the wedding luncheon, the parents of the bride and groom gave brief counsel to their children. Olivia was especially impressed when the bride's mother said, "My advice to you is short and sweet. Don't just be married. Be *very* married."

Olivia imagined that love, kindness, forgiveness, affection, and unwavering loyalty were all a big part of being *very* married. She couldn't wait to begin that journey with an eternal companion. And she thought Anthony might be just the man for the job.

On her flight back to Savona Springs, Olivia sat next to a friendly woman named Lauren.

"Do you live here in Salt Lake?" Lauren asked.

"No, I live in California. I was in town for my cousin's wedding."

"Are you married?"

"No, but I'm dating someone I really like. How about you?"

Lauren nodded. "I've been married for more than 20 years. I actually can't remember exactly how long. That's kind of embarrassing to admit, but the years just blend together. My husband and I have a 17-year-old son, a 14-year-old daughter, and an 11-year-old daughter."

She then retrieved a family photo from her purse and showed it to Olivia, who noticed that the woman's son was in a wheelchair. It also looked like he had a ventilator attached to his throat.

"I'm sure you're wondering why my son is in a wheelchair," said Lauren. "His name is Luke. A few years ago, he was hit by a car."

A wave of empathy touched Olivia heart.

"Luke was riding in the bike lane, but the driver drifted while she was staring at her phone. She was texting. She hit him from behind. By the time the car stopped, she'd run over him."

Lauren paused. "In a matter of seconds, he went from being a perfectly healthy teenager to being paralyzed from his diaphragm down. His goal had always been to play college basketball. Now, he has a motorized wheelchair and a ventilator breathes for him day and night."

"I'm very sorry," said Olivia.

"Luke may not be living the life I dreamed he would, but we're grateful he's still with us. He's getting good grades and is a great example to our family. But I'd give anything to trade places with him so that he could walk again, even if it were just for one day."

"How old was the driver who hit him?"

"She was 24. The judge sentenced her to two years in prison, but they released her after 16 months."

Lauren seemed lost in thought. She then continued. "I visited the girl while she was in prison. She cried and begged me to forgive her. I knew I needed to, but part of me felt that forgiving her would take away her responsibility for hurting Luke. It took me many months and countless prayers before I could honestly say I'd forgiven her. Forgiving her has blessed my life, her life, and my family's life."

"Wow," said Olivia. "I really admire you for that."

"We have so many things these days that distract us," Lauren said. "I see people driving on the freeway all the time and they're staring down at their phones. If they're driving 70 miles per hour, do you know how far they can go in just three seconds? Three hundred feet. That's the length of a football field.

"Before Luke's accident, he was a starter on the high school basketball team. His dream was to play for SSU. He still watches all their games."

"Does he have a favorite player?"

"He really likes watching Matt Schilling and Anthony Hull. I think those two guys play with the same kind of intensity that Luke used to."

"Anthony is actually a close friend of mine. I'm sure he'd come visit your son if you'd like him to."

Lauren's face lit up. "That'd be amazing, but I won't tell Luke until it's a done deal. I don't want him to get his hopes up. He's already had more than his share of disappointments."

The rhythmic sound of the ventilator was the first thing Anthony noticed as he entered Luke's bedroom. Olivia had called him right after returning from Utah, telling him about the paralyzed boy who was a big fan of SSU basketball. Anthony immediately called Lauren to set up a visit for that evening.

Luke broke into a smile as soon as he saw his visitor. Anthony was wearing his official Savona State University warm-up jacket. Luke partially lifted his right hand and gave Anthony a friendly fist bump.

"What's in the big…box?" Luke asked Anthony. Luke was able to speak quite well using the ventilator, but sometimes needed to pause between words.

"I brought you some gifts from the team."

Anthony then gave Luke a warm-up jacket, a basketball signed by all of the players and coaches, and a jersey with Anthony's number on it.

"Thanks!" Luke exclaimed. "This is crazy."

"I know you watch all of the SSU games," said Anthony. "From now on, the first time I shoot a free throw in a game, I'm going to brush the right side of my face with my hand. That'll be a signal just between you and me. My way of saying thanks for supporting me and the team."

"That would be…awesome," Luke said.

"Here's one more gift for you, by the way. It's a DVD with a bunch of SSU basketball highlights from the last 10 years."

"Can we watch it together?" Luke asked.

"Sure. Let's fire it up."

Soon after Anthony and Luke started watching the highlight reel, Luke's dad arrived home. He expressed gratitude for Anthony's visit and sat down to join them in front of the TV.

Driving home that evening, Anthony pondered how different life would be for Luke and his parents if that driver had just kept her eyes on the road. Although some people would describe Luke as an accident victim, Anthony saw it differently. The driver might not have hit Luke intentionally, but she'd made the decision to look at her phone.

Years earlier, Anthony had committed to never send or read texts while driving. And he'd kept that promise. From his point of view, it was no different than making a promise to never smoke and or drink alcohol.

44

The following morning, Anthony called Olivia. "I had a really good visit with Luke. I'm glad you met his mom on that flight. I think Luke and I are gonna be good friends."

"I'm so glad to hear that!" she said.

He could hear the smile in Olivia's voice.

He loved her smile.

# Chapter 10
## *Mamma's Place*

"So, this is where your parents had their first date," Olivia said as she and Anthony entered Mamma's Place.

"It's my all-time favorite restaurant. Whenever I come here, I think of my mom and dad falling in love."

When the headwaiter informed them that the restaurant was completely booked for the evening, Olivia noticed Anthony's look of disappointment. She had discovered long ago that it never hurts to ask, so she smiled at the headwaiter and said, "My boyfriend's mom worked here as a waitress 30 years ago. This is where she first met his dad. We'd be happy to wait until someone with a reservation is a no-show. I've never eaten here, but people say it's the best food in town."

The headwaiter returned her smile. "I'll see what I can do, but it might be a while."

In less than 10 minutes, they were seated at a nice table for two.

Anthony was amazed. "How did you do that?"

"I just asked nicely," she said. "Usually works like a charm."

"It probably has more to do with how *charming* you are. I doubt I could've gotten that guy to help us, regardless of how nice I was."

She smiled. "Thanks, but I think it works for anyone who asks kindly and politely."

"Well, this is definitely a place where kindness goes a long way. Remember how my dad stole my mom's heart by leaving big tips and being so nice to all of the servers?"

"It sounds like he was incredibly generous."

"Yes, my dad was a generous person," replied Anthony. "Almost to a fault."

After they placed their orders, he took Olivia by the hand and said, "I want to invite you to something amazing."

She lit up. "Tell me more."

"Have you heard of Dexter Mix?"

"The name sounds familiar."

"He's one of the richest people in town. Last year he gave something like $25 million to the Children's Hospital, and he makes donations to lots of other charitable causes. The Chamber of Commerce is honoring him next month with its *Giant of the City* award. Mr. Mix offered to pick up the entire tab for the event, including the food. He's a huge SSU basketball fan and we've become good friends. So, he invited me to come. And I get to bring a plus one."

In a ridiculous British accent, Anthony then said, "My darling, would you please join me at the upcoming *Giant of the City* gala? It will be maaaaaarvelous."

"I would love to be your date, my dear," she replied in a British accent that was much more pleasing to the ear.

"Awesome! It should be a blast. And it'll give me a break from my new roommate. He talks about himself nonstop. Honestly, he never stops. It's driving me crazy."

"Sometimes I worry I talk too much," said Olivia. "Please tell me if you think I'm ever rambling. It won't hurt my feelings."

"Trust me, Olivia, you don't talk too much. You have this nice way of gracefully moving from one topic to another. And your voice is so calm and soothing."

She smiled. "It's nice of you to say that."

After his date with Olivia, Anthony decided to spend the night at his mom's house.

"So, how are things going with you two?" his mom asked the following morning during breakfast.

"Every time I'm with her, I find something new that makes me like her even more."

His mom smiled and said, "If you fall in love with Olivia, and if she falls in love with you, the two of you will start seeing each other through the eyes of love. When that happens, it's wonderful."

# Chapter 11
## *People are Complicated*

"People are complicated," Chelsea Martin said to the other ward council members still standing around the glowing campfire. "My sister loves skydiving but has a phobia about speaking in public. I don't understand how giving a talk could ever be scarier than jumping out of an airplane."

Ty nodded his head and said, "We all have different fears. And we don't get to choose them. It almost seems like our fears choose us. I'm like your sister. I can go skydiving and rock climbing, but I don't like speaking in church."

Ty's roommate, Carson Lake, then shared his greatest fear. "I hate tight spaces. I'm claustrophobic. When I was a kid, I was in a crowded elevator and it got stuck between floors. We were packed in like sardines for almost an hour. I started hyperventilating. Then I puked. Now I always take the stairs."

After breakfast the following morning, the ward council members attended workshops, followed by a talk from Bishop Martin. He thanked them for their service and shared a simple idea that had made a positive difference in his life.

"Six months ago, my wife and I started keeping a gratitude journal," he explained. "Every night, we write down one or two specific things for which we were grateful that day. In our lives, we see what we're looking for. Our gratitude journals help us to look for and appreciate our blessings each day."

The bishop then turned the time over to his wife, who told an inspiring story of integrity.

"During the sixteenth century, King Henry VIII of England wanted to divorce his wife in order to marry Anne Boleyn. The Roman Catholic Church wouldn't condone this action, so the king started his own

48

church. The king required his subjects to take an oath of succession confirming his right to reign as the spiritual leader over the people of England.

"Sir Thomas More refused to take the oath, because it violated his conscience. By taking the oath, he would have joined countless other Englishmen who disagreed with what Henry VIII had done, but who were afraid to defy the king. More believed it was his sacred duty to follow his convictions, regardless of the actions of others. It's been said that no snowflake in an avalanche ever feels responsible, but More refused to utter the oath and join the avalanche.

"Sir Thomas More's silence thundered throughout Europe. When he refused to agree with the king, he was imprisoned in the Tower of London. And he became a martyr when he was beheaded by order of the king.

"As young adults, you don't face the risk of being killed by a power-hungry king. But you still face a wide variety of challenges and risks. Like Sir Thomas More, we need to maintain our integrity. We need to follow the teachings of our Savior with love, courage, faith, and conviction."

At the conclusion of the campout, Chelsea offered Ty and Carson a ride home. They both gladly accepted her offer. She was an attractive girl and both of them had independently thought about asking her out on a date at some point.

Her car was an old, red Dodge Charger. The air conditioning and driver's side seat belt were broken, but everything else seemed to work just fine. Since it was a hot day, they rolled down the windows for their drive out of the canyon.

Ty sat in front with Chelsea, while Carson rode in the back. After several minutes of small talk, Ty and Chelsea heard the sound of snoring coming from the back seat.

"Looks like little Carson's all tuckered out," Ty said with a smile.

After another few minutes, during a lapse in the conversation, Ty also fell asleep. Chelsea felt drowsy but wasn't too worried. In all her years of driving, she'd never fallen asleep at the wheel.

To stay awake, she put her head out of the window for a short time, which made her think of her dog, Lucy. She then turned on some music. She kept the volume low at first, but then turned it up to ward off the drowsiness. She assumed the louder music would wake Carson and Ty, but they both slept on.

To keep her mind active, she made a mental list of the five cutest guys in her ward. Looking over at Ty, she ranked him as *numero uno*. And

Carson took the third spot. She hoped that Carson would ask her out. Ty was a good guy but was a little arrogant for her taste. Carson was humbler and a better listener. She felt comfortable when she was with him. If Carson didn't ask her out within the next few weeks, she decided she'd have to take matters into her own hands.

Chelsea was now driving along a serpentine stretch of road by Pine Lake. While there was no guardrail between the road and the lake, a wide gravel shoulder provided a significant safety buffer. Beyond the shoulder, a rocky cliff dropped straight into the water about 15 feet below.

Despite the music and her confidence, Chelsea gradually dozed off. The road ahead curved sharply, and her car sped across the gravel shoulder. She woke just as the car plunged over the edge. Her horrified scream then jolted Carson and Ty from their slumber.

Because Chelsea's seat belt was broken, her forehead forcefully struck the windshield on impact, leaving her dazed. Ty quickly released his own seat belt and exited through the window. As he swam to the other side of the car to check on Chelsea, he noticed that the car's front end was beginning to sink.

In the meantime, Carson also climbed out through an open window. Ty, an exceptionally strong swimmer, could see that Carson was struggling.

"Kick off your shoes and swim toward the shore!" yelled Ty. "I'll take care of Chelsea."

As he looked at her through the driver's side window, Ty was startled to see a large gash on Chelsea's forehead. She stared back at him with a blank expression.

Reaching into the car, Ty took hold of Chelsea's upper arms and pulled her out. She didn't resist his efforts. He tried putting her on his back while he swam, but she repeatedly wrapped her arms tightly around his neck, making it difficult for him to stay afloat.

He moved her off his back, grabbed a handful of her long hair, and began towing her toward dry land.

"Does that hurt?" he asked.

"Not really," she muttered. "Maybe just a little bit."

Since there were only rocky cliffs in front of him, Ty had to drag Chelsea parallel to the shore for about 200 feet before reaching a small beach.

He could see that Carson was already sitting on the beach. He then noticed his bishop was there, as well. The Martins had been traveling right behind them and witnessed Chelsea's car plummeting into the lake. Sister Martin had already called for an ambulance.

As Ty swam toward the beach, the water quickly became shallower. He cradled Chelsea in his arms and carried her the rest of the way to safety. Bishop Martin snapped photos with his camera to document the dramatic scene.

Ty heard the sound of the approaching ambulance and two paramedics soon rushed down to the beach to examine Chelsea.

"We need to get that cut stitched up right away," explained one of the paramedics. "We'll take her to the hospital and make sure she doesn't have internal injuries. My hunch is that she's gonna be okay."

As she lay in her hospital bed, Chelsea felt tired but alert. When she saw Ty enter the room, she quickly stood up and gave him a long and grateful hug.

Her frantic parents arrived a few minutes later. They were relieved to see that Chelsea was in good spirits and profusely thanked Ty for his heroics.

In the end, Chelsea got a clean bill of health and went home from the hospital just a few hours after she was admitted.

# Chapter 12
## *No Greater Love*

On Monday morning, the *Savona Springs Gazette* published an article about Chelsea's rescue. The story featured one of Bishop Martin's photos of Ty carrying Chelsea in his arms toward the safety of the shore. It quickly became one of the most popular articles that had ever run on the *Gazette's* website.

Every attorney and staff member at Parks & Lane visited Ty's office to congratulate him. Many commented on the photo. One of the female attorneys said it was a scene right out of Hollywood and that he looked like a movie star.

Ty wanted to prominently display the photo in his office, but also didn't want to appear too self-promoting. He decided to get it framed immediately, then wait a week or so to hang it on the wall.

Olivia was shocked to see the photo of Ty as she browsed the news in her office at The Melby Foundation.

*It's great that he saved that girl,* she thought. *But he was far from a hero in the way he treated me.*

Later that day, Olivia considered sending Ty a congratulatory note. It would be a great way to take the high road. Ultimately, she decided against it because she didn't want Ty thinking she was still interested in him.

A saying came to her mind. *Hurt me once, shame on you. Hurt me twice, shame on me.*

"Did you see the crazy photo of Ty?" she asked her parents later that evening.

"Sure did," replied her dad. "I hated the way Ty treated you, but I have to give him credit. He did a great thing in helping that girl. Reading that story actually brought back painful memories of the bus crash. And Bella. Some people make the ultimate sacrifice."

Olivia and her parents sat in thoughtful silence, remembering Bella.

Her dad finally said, "We read a story last week about another person who gave their life to help others live. A plane had taken off from an airport back east. Because of ice buildup on the wings, it crashed into the Potomac River. Most of the passengers died on impact. Those who were still alive struggled in the icy water.

"A rescue helicopter came and lowered a rope down to the water. One passenger grabbed the rope and gave it to someone else, who was lifted into the helicopter. Each time the rope was lowered, this same man gave the rope to someone else. When the rope was lowered for the last time, the passenger who had passed the rope to others had disappeared under the water."

Olivia wiped tears from her cheeks. "What a tragic story."

"I found it inspiring," said her mother. "I thought of Bella searching the bus to make sure no student had been left behind. And I remembered the Savior's words: *Greater love hath no man than this, that he lay down his life for his friends.* That's what the Savior did for all of us."

On Wednesday morning, Ty cleared the north wall of his office to make way for his new favorite photo. He located a stud in the wall before pounding in the nail. With the added weight of the large frame, he wanted to be sure the photo was safely mounted.

He was out for lunch when two young attorneys stopped by his office to take a look. "Looks like Ty wants the world to know he saved that girl," one of the attorneys said. "I mean, who frames a photo of themselves like that? It's so arrogant."

"I don't mind it," replied the other attorney. "He saved someone's life. That should give you a free pass to gloat."

His fellow attorney paused for several moments. He then nodded in agreement. "I guess you're right. And, I have to admit, he looks pretty amazing in that picture. I'm probably just jealous."

# Chapter 13
## *Paradise Found*

Over the next two months, Olivia and Anthony saw each other nearly every day. The only exceptions were when he had away games. She loved his optimism and his gentle nature. He loved her kindness and the way she joyfully embraced life. With each week, his affection for her grew deeper.

They went on hikes in all three of the canyons east of Savona Springs. Her favorite was Kimball Canyon. His was Prospector's Canyon. They also ran together often at Veteran's Park. He marveled at her grace and speed.

When they weren't outdoors, they enjoyed spending time in the library. He worked on class assignments, while she read carefully selected books. They discussed Gospel topics for hours on end.

Although Olivia and Anthony expressed love for each other daily, she made it clear that she didn't want Anthony to move things along too quickly. Her painful experience with Ty had made her feel more cautious and vulnerable. Anthony tried to respect her wishes, but he had already come to the conclusion that Olivia was remarkable.

Like all courtships, theirs had its imperfections. Both of them had quirks and they dealt with occasional misunderstandings. But they were good about not treating the little things like big things.

Olivia had always felt that Anthony was cute, but somehow his inner goodness made his outward appearance even more attractive as she came to know him better.

On Valentine's Day, he invited her to dinner at a nice restaurant. When she appeared at her front door wearing a striking dress, Anthony was stunned.

"Wow," he gushed. "You look beautiful."

To both their surprise, tears began to roll down Olivia's cheeks. Perhaps she was crying because Anthony had looked at her in such an adoring way. Or maybe the tears came because he was the first guy who ever told her that she looked beautiful and she knew in her heart he meant every word.

The following night, they picked up Grandma Angela and attended a play about the Civil War. The story followed the wartime experiences of three fictional soldiers. Two fought for the North and one for the South. All three were married and they suffered greatly. One lost a leg but survived. One had a severe emotional breakdown but later recovered. The third soldier never returned to his wife and children—he had perished in battle.

When the curtain came down, Anthony, Olivia, and Angela felt a wave of compassion for those who die in war and the loved ones who have to go on without them.

The following evening, Anthony joined Olivia and her parents for dinner. Her dad asked Anthony if there was something in particular that motivated him during basketball games.

"Before every game, I always say the same thing to myself. It's a quote from Winston Churchill. *Never, never, never give up.*"

"That's exactly how I feel about my patients," Olivia's dad replied. "I've learned to never give up on them. I've seen patients come back from the brink of death to enjoy long and healthy lives. And I feel that way about the young adults in my ward. Since I became a bishop, I've thought a lot about the parable of the prodigal son. I love that the father didn't just wait to welcome back his wayward son. He ran to greet him when he was still afar off. He never gave up on his child. I know our Father in Heaven never gives up on us."

"So true," said Anthony. "Speaking of never giving up during tough times, Olivia told me that you were in Manhattan on September 11."

"Yes, I was in the city for a medical seminar. My hotel was less than a mile from the Twin Towers. It was a beautiful morning. While I was watching the news in my room, I heard a faint boom and the windows rattled.

"The reporters on TV thought that a small plane had accidentally hit one of the towers. When the second plane hit the other tower, it became clear that it was a coordinated attack.

"I tried to call my wife, but all the circuits were busy. She was frantically trying to reach me, and I was frantically trying to reach her. I felt restless, so I left my hotel and went down to the street to get a better feel for what was happening. I saw fire trucks speeding down the street heading to the Twin Towers. They kept coming and coming, with sirens blazing. I saw at least 30 fire trucks on that one street. Many of the firefighters looked so very young. I feared for their safety.

"I walked toward the Twin Towers. When I was about five blocks away, I watched as fire and smoke poured out of those massive 110-story buildings. Suddenly, the south tower collapsed into a pile of destruction. It had never crossed my mind that the towers might come down.

"About 40 minutes later, the north tower also crumbled. It seemed like a terrible dream. I was walking back to my hotel when a call finally came through from my wife. Her voice sounded like the voice of an angel. She and the children were greatly relieved to know I was safe. Talking with her, a feeling of peace came into my heart.

"After a great deal of effort, I finally found a hotel in upper Manhattan. All taxis and private cars had been banned from the area, so I had to walk more than 50 blocks to my new hotel. The only vehicles authorized to drive that day were police cars, ambulances, fire trucks, and military vehicles. I saw several Army tanks moving along the avenues of upper Manhattan. It was surreal to see tanks driving on the streets of New York City.

"When I reached my hotel, the workers were making people wait outside. Only a small number of people at a time were allowed to enter the lobby. I stood outside for more than two hours before I was able to check into my room. I turned on the TV and it was absolutely heartbreaking. Many channels were posting photos of missing people.

"Although I'd felt incredibly sad all day, I hadn't yet cried. I was still in a state of shock. But seeing photo after photo of so many missing persons, the tears finally came. I desperately wanted to go home. But air traffic was grounded, and no one knew when flights would resume. Some people were saying it would be a week. I wanted to rent a car and drive to Savona Springs, but no rental cars were available.

"My wife came up with a creative idea. She called a car rental company in Connecticut. They had one car left. As I started driving west from Connecticut, our oldest son drove from California to meet me halfway. I saw American flags everywhere. They were hanging from homes and overpasses and barns and billboards and skyscrapers.

"After two long days of driving, my son and I met at the Nauvoo Temple, which was still under construction. We knelt next to our car and prayed for all our family members. We prayed for those who had been injured or had lost loved ones. When we finally reached Savona Springs, I felt incredibly grateful to be home, safe and sound, with the family I love."

"Looking back, what's the biggest thing you learned from that experience?" asked Anthony.

Olivia's dad was quiet as he collected his thoughts. "It was a powerful reminder of what is truly important in life. On the night of September 11, when I spent hours watching TV, I didn't see any photos of expensive cars. Nobody said, 'Please call immediately if you have seen this car.' There were *no* photos of material possessions. They were photos of missing people who were deeply loved. That day strengthened my belief that our lives should be centered on the people we love. Life is about relationships. We need to always make time for the people we love most."

The final basketball game of Anthony's college career was a real barnburner. He logged 21 points and eleven rebounds, and even managed to remain in the game until the final buzzer. His aggressive style of play had led him to foul out more than a few times that season.

In recognition of his accomplishments, Anthony was voted conference player of the year. This award was particularly impressive, considering his team had been consistently mediocre, falling just short of a winning record.

Because he was a superb high school basketball player, the SSU coaches had assumed that he'd enroll in a college with a better program. The truth was that he only chose SSU in order to stay near his widowed mom. He wanted to help her, spend time with her, and make it so she could see his games. And she never once missed a home game. She was his biggest fan.

Anthony was happy that his mom had recently started dating a man she'd known in high school nearly 40 years earlier. They'd been good friends during all three years of school, and he'd actually taken her to senior prom. He had lost his wife to cancer. They were now going out together twice a week. His mom wasn't sure yet if she wanted to remarry, but she enjoyed his company.

As Anthony slept at his mom's home that night after his last college game, he had a troubling dream. He dreamed that he was the only person in Savona Springs. Every other man, woman, and child had somehow disappeared. The city had become a wasteland.

Anthony didn't want to be alone.

# Chapter 14
## *A Man Divided*

Early Monday morning, Ty entered the lobby of Parks & Lane. A few seconds later, a beautiful girl appeared and smiled in his direction. She had light blue eyes and thick red hair.

"Hi, I'm Allison Adams," she said. "I'm the new receptionist."

"Nice to meet you, Allison. My name's Ty. I'm one of the newer attorneys here. I passed the bar last summer and started working here in August."

After another moment of small chat, Ty waved goodbye and headed for his office. But a mere five minutes later, Allison knocked on his half-opened door.

"Come on in," he said with a smile. "Please have a seat."

As she sat down, she said, "I hear you graduated from BYU Law."

"Sure did."

"Are you a member of the LDS Church?"

"I am. How about you, Allison?"

"Yep. I just returned a few months ago from my mission in Alaska."

"Awesome," he replied. "I served in Denmark."

She then looked at the large photo displayed on his wall. "Love that picture. I hear you saved her life."

"I was just in the right place at the right time."

"I think it was a bit more than that," she said. "From that photo on your desk, it looks like when you're not saving damsels in distress, you also go skydiving."

"Yeah, that was fun. Have you ever tried it?"

"No, but I'd love to sometime."

Ty immediately liked Allison's adventuresome side. He had no idea that Allison's family lived next door to the firm's managing partner, Fletcher Parks. The two families were close friends. After Allison returned from her mission, Fletcher had offered her the receptionist job. Her bright mind and gregarious personality made her a natural for the position.

As she was leaving Ty's office, Allison said, "Mr. Parks wants you to join him for a meeting with a client at 10:00 in the small conference room."

"I'll be there. Thanks, Allison!"

Born into a wealthy family, Ty had snorkeled in the crystal waters of Tahiti, walked along the Great Wall of China, and skied in the Swiss Alps before graduating high school. He had two sisters, one seven years older than Ty, the other six years older. His parents had hoped for another child after the girls were born but had concluded that it probably wouldn't happen. They were surprised and thrilled when Ty arrived.

His sisters both married when he was a teenager. As a wedding gift, they each recieved a $100,000 check from Ty's parents to help with a down payment on their first home. Before his mission, his father assured Ty that he'd receive a similar check when he married.

Ten days after he returned from Denmark, his dad told Ty that a severe economic downturn had devastated his business. Looking sad and weary, his dad said, "My business is bankrupt."

Ty was shocked. "Do you still have the money set aside for me when I get married?"

"When my business went under, I lost everything. I'm so sorry."

"It isn't fair that the girls got that money and I get nothing. Shouldn't they at least give me some of the money that you gave to them?

His dad looked a little surprised. "I wish I could turn back the clock, but I can't. My business was going great back then and they've already used the money on their homes. It wouldn't be fair to ask for it now."

Ty was frustrated that his dad hadn't planned better, but also felt sorry for him. His dreams must have been dashed when the business failed. On top of that, his dad was diabetic and was having problems with his kidneys.

After a long pause, Ty said, "Don't worry about the money. I'll be fine. I appreciate the way you paid for my mission and my first year of college and took me on such great vacations growing up. I'm sorry about your business, and I'm sorry that you're having medical problems. I know you'd help me if you had the money."

Four months after discovering he wouldn't be getting the same wedding gift his sisters received, Ty learned his dad needed a kidney transplant. His dad wept when Ty volunteered to be a donor. Testing revealed his kidney would be a good match.

The transplant was successful, and his dad's health greatly improved. It had actually been a blessing for Ty, because he felt better about himself after making such a dramatic difference in the life of someone he loved.

Ty gazed out at Savona Springs from the conference room window as he waited for Fletcher to arrive. *I like living here*, he thought. *It's beautiful, and the people are so friendly*. His thoughts drifted to Olivia. She'd been born and raised here, and really put Savona Springs on the map for him.

Their first date was back in December. By mid-January, they were dating exclusively. On a night in early June, he'd come *oh so close* to proposing to her, but changed his mind at the last minute. Then his romantic attraction for Olivia started to fade a bit. The spark wasn't totally dead. It simply didn't burn as brightly as before.

Twenty-seven-year-old Ty had established a pattern of losing interest in girls after dating them for several months. He decided to stop dating Olivia on Independence Day during the Stadium of Fire celebration in Provo.

He had learned from sad experience that breaking up is hard no matter how gently you try to do it. Shortly before he met Olivia, he'd ended things with a girl named Heather. His break-up talk with her was an absolute train wreck. She asked him lots of questions and his off-the-cuff answers only seemed to make her feel worse.

*Rejection is rejection*, he thought. *Best to just rip off the band-aid.*

Because his talk with Heather went so poorly, Ty made a decision. The next time he stopped dating a girl, he'd just disappear. And that was exactly how he broke up with Olivia. After dating her for seven months, he left without attempting any kind of explanation.

He loved her, but just not quite enough to marry her.

Before his mission, Ty decided to become a high school basketball coach. A fast and strong point guard, he had led his high school team to the state semi-finals. He believed his talents would make him an excellent coach.

But plans change. With no hope of receiving financial help from his parents, Ty decided that he needed a career with more earning potential. With a growing mountain of student loan debt, he considered a variety of options. Ultimately, he enrolled at the BYU Law School because it seemed like his best opportunity to have the lifestyle he wanted.

Looking back, he often wondered if he'd made the right decision. He should have been getting into a groove at Parks & Lane by now, but he still felt like he was drowning.

Ty worked longer hours than he preferred and his supervising partner, Rex, was gloomy, unfriendly, and demanding. He could brighten a room just by leaving it. But even if Rex weren't in the picture, Ty didn't want to spend most of his waking hours for the next 40 years inside an office. In his heart, he wanted to leave the legal profession, go back to college, and become a high school coach.

The logical part of him knew that leaving the firm wasn't a financially viable option in light of his lack of savings and substantial student loan debt. Ty wasn't living the life he wanted, but he couldn't think of a better option.

# Chapter 15
## *Totally in the Dark*

Ty stood up promptly when Fletcher entered the room. Fletcher was short but strong, with a shaved head and a deeply resonant voice that reminded Ty of the actor Morgan Freeman.

Fletcher was also smart and friendly, with a dazzling ability to remember names and faces.

"In a few minutes, I'll be meeting with a client named Ezra Harris," Fletcher told Ty. "I thought it would be a good learning experience for you to sit in on the meeting. Ezra is in his 90s and his health is starting to go downhill. He has an old will that he wants to revise."

Before long, Allison gracefully entered the conference room with Ezra. She flashed a smile at Ty.

"Good morning, Ezra," Fletcher said. "I've invited one of our newer attorneys, Ty Bradwell, to join us, if that's all right with you."

Ezra smiled and said, "Fine by me. It's nice to meet you, Ty."

"Nice to meet you, Mr. Harris."

Fletcher reviewed the documents arranged on his desk. "Ezra, you told me on the phone that your wife passed away two years ago and that you have one child."

"Yes, Mary is my only living child. My wife had two miscarriages during our marriage. We also had a daughter named Linda, who died from polio when she was four. That polio was a terrible disease. She was placed in an iron lung for several months. Broke my heart when we lost her."

Ty noticed that Ezra's eyes were rimmed with tears as he recalled his daughter who had passed away so many years ago.

"Three years after Linda passed away, Mary was born," Ezra continued. "Our joy was overwhelming. Mary is an angel. She helps me so much."

"Ezra, help me understand more about your financial situation," Fletcher said.

"I own my house free and clear. It's worth about $600,000. I have no debts and, thanks to my parents, I'm much richer than I ever expected to be."

*This is getting interesting*, Ty thought as he leaned forward.

"About 50 years ago, my parents purchased some desert land. I can't remember exactly how many acres. They paid very little because the land was so far away from city limits. It was definitely out in the boondocks. My dad died first, about six years before my mom. Savona Springs kept growing and growing, and the land kept increasing in value. When my mom died, my sister and I each got half of the property."

Ezra started to cough. He took a drink of water and then continued. "My sister and I decided to hold onto the land since it was still going up in value. Last year, we both finally decided to sell. Our patience paid off, because we ended up getting $9 million each."

*Wow*, Ty thought.

"In the first will that I signed after my wife died, I left everything to Mary. In this new will, the first gift is $3 million to Mary. She also gets my house, my car, and all of my other personal property."

Ezra's coughing returned, so Ty poured him another glass of water.

"After Mary receives her inheritance, each of my three grandchildren will receive a million. I'm so proud of my grandchildren. They are all hard workers and I want to give them a strong financial safety net. You never know what might happen. Things are getting more expensive and life can change in a heartbeat. One of my neighbors had a son who contracted some rare disease. He was in the hospital for months. His family's share of the bill was more than $700,000, even though they had health insurance."

Ezra was then silent for at least a full minute. Fletcher and Ty both wondered if he might be feeling ill. When he spoke again, it was slower and more labored. "The rest of my money will be split equally between LDS Charities and an organization that helps amputees. I forgot its name, but I'll call you with it after I get home. I lost my left hand in World War II, so amputees are near and dear to my heart."

"It's great that so many advances are being made in prosthetics these days," Fletcher said.

"Yes, it's truly amazing," replied Ezra. "I think I have given you all the information you need to revise my will. If you don't mind indulging a proud grandpa, here's a photo of me with my grandchildren."

He handed the photo to Fletcher, who looked at it and said, "They look like some great kids."

Fletcher then passed the photo to Ty. After a quick glance, Ty was left speechless. He blinked and stared at the photo again. Olivia stood in the middle, with her arm around Grandpa Ezra Harris. They were flanked by Olivia's two brothers.

Ty quickly made a decision. He wasn't going to tell Ezra that he had dated Olivia.

"I have always been private about my finances," Ezra said. "My daughter will be shocked when she learns how much money she will inherit."

Ezra smiled. "I also wish that I could see the reaction of my grandchildren when my will is read and they each get $1 million. They will be surprised. I wonder how much we get to see of this world after we have gone on to the next."

"I've wondered that myself," Fletcher said. "And these changes aren't complicated, Ezra. We can have your revised will ready for you to sign by 5:00 tonight."

"Great. At my age, I want to sign it as soon as possible."

Fletcher then escorted Ezra to the elevator. When he returned to the conference room, Ty asked him if Ezra's grandchildren would need to pay taxes on their inheritance.

"No, their inheritances will be tax-free. Ezra's estate will pay the estate taxes to the extent any such taxes are due. Just so we're clear, Ty, this matter is strictly confidential. I only brought you in as a learning opportunity. Don't discuss it with anyone."

As Fletcher left the conference room, he noticed that Ezra had accidently left his family photo on the conference room table. Fletcher picked it up so he could return it to Ezra later that afternoon. Gazing intently at the photo, his eyes were drawn to Olivia. She was wearing a white baseball cap that had the word "Italia" written on it. *Strange,* Fletcher thought. *I never would've imagined that baseball was popular in Italy.*

When he arrived for work that morning, Ty had no plans to ever date Olivia again. Of course, there were times when he missed being with her. But now that he knew about her future inheritance, he was ready to take a fresh look at things.

*A million would be incredible,* he thought. *That's ten times more than my selfish sisters got. Maybe life isn't so unfair after all.*

He decided that he needed to talk to Fletcher right away.

"May I ask you a question?" he said, poking his head into Fletcher's office.

"Sure. Have a seat."

"I think you should know something," Ty began. "More than a year ago, I started dating Ezra Harris' granddaughter, Olivia. We were at BYU. I had no idea Ezra was her grandfather until the end of the meeting today, when he passed around that photo."

Ty noticed the concerned look on Fletcher's face.

"So, are you telling me that you dated Ezra Harris' granddaughter in Provo, but you are no longer interested in her?"

"No," said Ty, choosing his words carefully. "That's not what I'm saying. A few days before Christmas, Olivia moved here from Provo. My plan was to ask her out again right after the holidays, but she went on a long trip to England. I think she gets back in a few days. I'm going to ask her out as soon as she gets back."

Ty knew that Olivia had already returned from her trip, because he'd seen her at the recent SSU Institute fireside. But he considered that an inconvenient little detail.

"So, to be clear, you already planned to ask Olivia out again before you learned about her inheritance today?"

"Yes, I did. I love her. We dated for seven months in Provo. I'll definitely ask her out once she gets back from her trip."

Fletcher found comfort in Ty's explanation.

"Dating decisions are not law firm decisions," Fletcher said. "They're personal decisions. I have no problem with you dating Olivia, since you were already planning to ask her out before you learned about her inheritance. But you cannot tell Olivia, or anyone else, about her inheritance. That is strictly confidential."

Ty nodded in agreement. "I promise I won't say anything about her grandfather's will."

"And you are now out of the loop as far as Ezra's will is concerned," said Fletcher. "You will never be part of any meetings or conversations where it is discussed. Is that clear?"

"Yes, it's perfectly clear. Are you going to tell Ezra about this?"

Fletcher paused. "No. I don't think that would serve any purpose."

"If I'd known that Ezra was her grandfather, I totally would've left the meeting right away."

"I understand that," Fletcher said.

"Do you think Ezra is mentally sharp enough to revise his will?"

"Yes, he's clearly capable of revising his will. He could not remember exactly how many acres he had before he sold his land, but that doesn't make him incompetent. It's not uncommon for elderly clients to have a few memory issues."

Fletcher looked directly at Ty and said in a serious tone of voice, "You now know Olivia is going to inherit a large sum of money, but she doesn't know that. She also doesn't know that you know about her inheritance. That's not fair to her, but the situation is what it is."

"I understand," Ty said. He then returned to his office.

Fletcher had practiced law for more than 20 years and nothing like this had ever happened to him. It was an extraordinary coincidence and he felt badly for Olivia. If she started dating Ty again, he would have a distinct advantage in their relationship. Ty was walking in broad daylight, but she was totally in the dark.

When Fletcher was leaving the office late that afternoon, he stopped by Ty's office. "I want to remind you again that you can have no more involvement of any kind with Ezra's will. Is that clear?"

"Yes, it's perfectly clear," Ty replied.

Right before he went to bed that night, Ty began talking out loud to himself, which he often did when something was troubling him.

*Fletcher crossed the line today when he asked all about me dating Olivia. Who I choose to date and why I choose to date them is a private matter. He's my boss, but my dating decisions are none of his business.*

66

# Chapter 16
## *Not So Strictly Confidential*

Ty had been Carson Parks' trainer in the Denmark Copenhagen Mission. When Carson was a third-year medical student at SSU, he heard that Ty had accepted a job with a law firm in Savona Springs. Carson's current roommate was getting married and moving out, so he reached out to Ty, who was more than happy to take over the housing contract.

That summer, Ty moved into Carson's two-bedroom apartment. The former mission companions reminisced for hours about their experiences together.

"Have you ever come close to being engaged?" Carson asked one night.

"Just once. I almost proposed to a girl back in Provo. Maybe you know her, since you both grew up here. Her name is Olivia Michaels."

"Oh yeah, I actually know her fairly well," Carson said. "We were in the same stake and went to the same high school. I never dated her or anything, but I had a couple of classes with her. She's super smart. Why did you break up?"

"Good question. I loved her, but it just seemed like the relationship had run its course. Tough decision, though. How about you? Have you ever been engaged?"

"Nope," Carson said. "I've only been in a couple serious relationships. Got dumped both times. Probably on account of my body odor. Or maybe it's my pet ferrets. Who knows?"

More than eight months after that first conversation, Ty arrived at his apartment following the meeting with Ezra Harris. He was surprised to see Carson there, because medical school obligations usually kept him out much later.

"Do you remember when we talked last year about me dating Olivia Michaels?" Ty asked.

"Yeah."

"I need to tell you something about her, but it's strictly confidential."

"If the information's confidential, why are you telling me?"

Ty ignored Carson's comment and said, "I sat in on a meeting today with Olivia's grandpa. She's going to inherit $1 million when he dies. And I'm guessing he probably only has about three months to live, give or take."

Carson was stunned and disappointed. "Ty, you can't disclose confidential information like that. One of my classmates got kicked out of medical school just last month for passing on confidential patient information."

Ty seemed annoyed. "You're the only person I've told about Olivia's inheritance. I know you're really good about keeping things to yourself. Just don't tell anyone and there won't be a problem."

Carson had no desire to tell anyone about Olivia's future inheritance, but he was upset that Ty so openly discussed another person's private information.

"When I dated Olivia in Provo, I came close to proposing to her," Ty said. "I just couldn't get all of the way there. My dream is to be a high school basketball coach, but I have a ton of debt. High school coaches and teachers don't make much. Learning about Olivia's inheritance gives me that little push I needed to start dating her again. I need to think about it more. She was probably a little put out at the way things ended, but I bet she'd be happy to pick up where we left off."

Carson felt let down by the friend he'd once looked up to. He didn't know what to say, so he didn't say anything.

Ty broke the silence. "I'll give the relationship one more try. She's a wonderful person and I'll be careful not to hurt her again."

"Got it," said Carson. "Well, I've got to go run an errand."

Walking to his car, Carson fumed. Ty was acting selfishly at best and unethically at worst. In high school, Carson had learned the importance of confidentiality through a painful mistake. Near the end of his senior year, he was dating a girl named Lisa. They'd been very good friends since ninth grade but had only been dating each other for a few months.

One day, Lisa told Carson that she had a serious eating disorder and was going to enter a treatment facility right after graduation. To keep her disorder private, she was telling all her other friends that she was going to California to stay with her aunt.

"Please don't tell anyone," Lisa told him. "You're the only person outside my family who knows about this."

Carson promised that he'd keep her secret. One week after graduation, Lisa entered the clinic. Not long afterward, in a moment of weakness, Carson told another friend that Lisa was in a clinic that dealt with eating disorders. He immediately regretted spilling the beans and made his friend promise to not tell anyone else.

Sadly, the very next day his friend did exactly what Carson had done. He told just one other person about Lisa. But then that person told three other people, and those three people told other people, who then told even more people.

Carson later received a call from Lisa. She was sobbing. "I thought I could trust you. Now everybody knows I'm here. I can't believe you told people."

"I'm so sorry," he said. "I know I made a huge mistake, but I didn't tell everyone. I only told Mark. I promise it was just one person."

"Well, lots of other people know. And you're the only person I told. This is your fault."

Carson knew she was right. If he'd kept his promise, her secret would've stayed a secret. He still felt terrible about that experience. He learned that when you promise to keep something confidential, you make no exceptions. Tell even one person and you've lost all control of the situation.

In the military, they say that loose lips sink ships. Carson learned that loose lips also sink friendships. And now he was greatly troubled that Ty had told him all about Olivia's inheritance. It troubled him even more that Ty wanted to exploit his relationship with Olivia to gain access to that money.

# Chapter 17
## *Freedom to Choose*

Angela Michaels walked next door to the home of her best friend, Naomi Roth.

"Happy birthday," she said, holding out a birthday cake covered with chocolate frosting. "Sorry, but I didn't have 94 candles! I only had 20."

"Close enough," Naomi replied.

Angela and Naomi had lived next to each other for 30 years and were like two peas in a pod. They both loved tennis and played twice a week for many years, though Naomi's knee problems ended that tradition. Naomi lost her husband to a heart attack one year before Angela's husband also died from a heart attack. Both women had one child living in Savona Springs and two children living in faraway states. They were both religious. Naomi was Jewish and Angela was LDS. After decades as friends and neighbors, they felt like sisters.

In 1944, Naomi was living in Hungary with her family. They were arrested and sent to the infamous Auschwitz concentration camp, where they endured unspeakable physical, mental, and emotional misery.

One day, a prisoner escaped from Auschwitz. In a shockingly brutal effort to discourage future escapes, the camp leaders randomly chose ten innocent prisoners to be executed. None of those who were chosen had ever tried to escape. Naomi's 17-year-old brother was one of the prisoners murdered in retribution for a single prisoner's successful escape.

After two months in Auschwitz, the guards decided that Naomi's parents were too ill and weak to be productive workers, so they were both murdered in the camp's gas chamber. Barely out of her teenage years, Naomi was already an orphan and had lost her only sibling. Her aunt

Ruth, who had also been sent to Auschwitz, was her only remaining relative.

On a frigid night in 1945, Naomi and her aunt were sleeping in the same barrack when they were awakened by the sound of explosions. The Russian Army had almost reached Auschwitz, so the Nazi soldiers quickly forced everyone out of the barracks. The inmates were ordered to start marching down a dark road as the sounds of battle thundered around them.

The next three weeks of marching were absolutely brutal. Their thin concentration camp clothing was no match for the snow and wind. Severe hunger, thirst, fatigue, blisters, sickness, and bleeding feet were constant during their journey. Those who stopped to rest were often murdered by the guards.

When Naomi and Ruth arrived in Germany, they became forced laborers in a manufacturing plant. The hours were long and the shifts grueling. Just a few months later, the world finally changed. Hitler was dead, the Axis forces had surrendered, and Naomi and her aunt regained their precious freedom.

Naomi immigrated to New York City, where she met and married her husband. When their three children grew to be adults, they all moved to different cities. One son lived in Atlanta, another in Seattle, and one in Savona Springs. In 1984, Naomi and her husband also moved to Savona Springs.

Because of her close relationship with Naomi, Angela had read several books about the treatment of Jews during World War II. She was shocked to learn that at the start of the war, there were approximately nine million Jews in Europe. By the end of the war, about six million Jews had died, including one million children.

"I had a nightmare last night," Naomi told Angela. "I was back in the concentration camp. I was hungry and the lice were making me miserable."

"It must have been awful," Angela said tenderly. After more than 70 years, both women still had nightmares about their war experiences. Recently, Angela had dreamed again about the injured young soldier who repeatedly called out for his mom.

Angela told Naomi that she'd been asked to give a talk in her LDS ward in a few weeks. The assigned topic was "Acting for ourselves, rather than re-acting to others."

"If you reacted the wrong way to the concentration camp guards, they would shoot you," Naomi said.

"When my children were young, I always told them that we need to act for ourselves instead of reacting to what other people do or say," Angela said. "When we react, we are letting other people control us. We give away our God-given agency to make our own decisions and to choose our own path."

Naomi smiled. "Angela, we're a couple of old war horses, but I'm so glad we still have each other."

Angela then lit the candles on the cake and sang a Happy Birthday solo to Naomi, who blew out all of the candles after a couple of rigorous attempts.

"Would you like to have dinner with me on Sunday?" Naomi asked.

"I'd love to," replied Angela. "I'll bring a salad and dessert."

"Great. I'll see you Sunday at 2:00."

As she left Naomi's home, Angela had no way of knowing that her dear friend would pass away quietly in her sleep that night.

# Chapter 18
## *Lifting Feathers*

Earlier that day, Anthony had called his mom to let her know he'd be coming over. He tried to stay at his mom's house at least once or twice a week so she wouldn't be alone. He'd asked many times if she wanted him to move in with her, but his mom always declined his thoughtful offer.

Although Anthony didn't sing particularly well and could only plunk out a few simple songs on the piano, music kindled something special inside him. He didn't fully understand how or why music touched his heart and his soul so deeply, but he knew it made the world a better place.

"Mom, would you please sing a few hymns for me?"

"What do I look like, a jukebox?" she asked with a smile. "Just kidding. Of course, I'd be happy to."

For the next 20 minutes, she played a variety of hymns on both her piano and harp. Afterward, Anthony gave her a kiss on the cheek and headed off to bed.

Anthony had an early class, so he got ready before dawn. As he was about to leave, he stopped to look at the large family photo in the living room. It was a moment frozen in time. His family had gone to a professional studio because his mom wanted the photo done just right. It was taken shortly before his dad was deployed to Afghanistan.

Anthony loved the photo because his parents looked so happy and so much in love. He thought that his brother and sister also looked great in the photo. Their smiles were so relaxed. He disliked his own forced smile, the result of the photographer telling them all to say "cheese" right before the photo was taken.

*Everyone looks happy except me*, Anthony had thought the first time he saw the photo.

Two weeks before his dad left for Afghanistan, while the family was having dinner together, the subject of the photo came up. By now it had been framed and hung in the living room.

"I think it's a nice photo," Anthony said. "Sorry that my smile looks kind of weird."

His mom replied, "You look very handsome in the photo, but my hair isn't quite right."

"I look kind of sleepy in it," added his sister. "I hate the bags under my eyes."

His dad had heard enough.

"Lighten up everybody," his dad said with a smile. "This is a great family photo and I absolutely love it. Instead of focusing on what's wrong with it, think about what's right. We're all together. We're all healthy. We're all ridiculously good-looking. We all love each other. That's why I think this is such a great photo and that's why we should all thank Mom. Without her, this photo would never have happened."

Everyone then said in nearly perfect unison, "Thanks, Mom."

Anthony's dad was the most optimistic person he had ever known. He often told his children that they should love life and embrace its challenges as well as its joys. He told them that doing hard things makes you stronger and happier in the long run.

"You can't build muscle by lifting a feather," he'd say. "If we want to grow stronger physically and spiritually, we need to do things that stretch us."

Before leaving for class, Anthony wrote a note and placed it on the kitchen table.

*"Thanks for being the best mom ever. Your music was beautiful. Love you so much!"*

His mom smiled as she read his note during breakfast. She then read it a second time and placed it in the polished wooden box that held countless other notes Anthony and his siblings had written to her through the years.

The box also contained many precious notes and letters from her dear, departed husband.

# Chapter 19
## *The Rhythm of Life*

Lee Melby and his wife, Ann, invited Olivia and Anthony to join them at a sold-out performance of the Savona Springs Fine Arts Center's newest musical. The foursome enjoyed being together and all were touched by the performance's message of forgiving, forgetting, and moving forward.

Afterward, they walked out of the art center and into the pleasant evening. While Ann and Olivia chatted with each other, Lee said to Anthony, "Olivia's a smart and energetic employee, but that isn't what impresses me most about her. It's as if she is wearing some special type of contact lens that filters out the bad in others and leaves her seeing only the good."

"That's so true," agreed Anthony. "She's always quick to give people the benefit of the doubt. I sometimes worry that she trusts people too easily, but I guess that's better than judging too harshly."

After they said goodbye to Lee and Ann, Olivia sang one of the songs from the musical as the pair ambled around the parking lot looking for Anthony's car. He had a tendency to forget exactly where he'd parked, but neither of them minded taking the scenic route on such a beautiful night.

"I've always wished I could sing better," said Anthony. "But now I'm more than happy to just listen to you."

She smiled and softly said, "Thanks. I love that you enjoy it when I sing to you. For me, music is like the sun and the stars. It makes the world more beautiful. It's a language that touches our heart and our soul like nothing else can."

Eventually, they found Anthony's car right where he left it. As they drove toward home, Anthony said something that Olivia found inspiring.

"I love the rhythm and the seasons of life. I love how the sun rises and sets every day. Without darkness, we'd never see the stars. Without darkness, we'd never fully appreciate the light."

Olivia smiled. After a rather long pause, she said, "Don't you sometimes feel sad that time is passing by too quickly? Don't you sometimes wish that you were 18 again and just starting college?"

Anthony nodded. "Every year, time seems to move faster. When I was in junior high, time seemed to last forever. But my mission and college years have sped by. Only my history teacher has the power to make time stand still. His lectures drag on *forever*. But when I'm with you for an hour, it seems like ten minutes."

"That's sweet," she replied. "Time really does fly by when we're together."


Ty had also attended the musical that night. His date was a tall girl named Natalie. She was a nurse, a runner, and a member of the ward Ty attended. This was their fifth date together and Ty felt things were going well.

As Ty and Natalie were leaving the Fine Arts Center, an older woman approached him. She was wearing a diamond necklace and a yellow gown that showed off her alarmingly dark tan.

Ty couldn't help but wonder if the woman had ever heard of sunscreen.

"Excuse me," said the woman. "May I ask you a question?"

"Sure, go ahead."

"My name is Millicent Argyle. My husband and I own an ad agency in Los Angeles. We're helping a client launch a new cologne called Truly Blue. The advertising campaign will feature a male model. He must have vivid blue eyes and he needs to be good-looking in a mysterious sort of way."

She then carefully studied Ty's facial features and his remarkable blue eyes.

"We've already done photo shoots of seven different models in LA, but our client doesn't feel that we've found the right person."

Millicent then looked Ty over one last time and said, "With that dimple in your chin and those stunning eyes, I think you might be the man we're looking for. Would you be willing to come in for a photo shoot?"

Ty was flattered. "How long will it take?"

"No more than thirty minutes. We'll pay you for your time, of course. And if you're selected as the model, you'll be paid quite well."

76

Ty wanted to ask just what "quite well" meant, but he decided he could find out later. He instead said, "Sure, I could do a photo shoot."

"Would Thursday night at 7:00 work for you?"

"That works fine."

Millicent gave him the address to the studio. Ty then took hold of Natalie's hand as they continued on their way down the sidewalk.

"Don't let that little chat go to your head, Mr. Truly Blue," Natalie said with a smile. "It does sound like a pretty cool opportunity, though. And speaking of work, are things at the firm going any better for you?"

"Not really. I'm still working longer hours than I'd like. I was at the office last Saturday for at least three or four hours. And I can't stand my supervisor. He's one of those super grumpy people you hate to be around."

"Sorry to hear it," Natalie said. "It's no fun when work is such a drag."

The following day, Ty called Natalie and invited her to dinner. He was disheartened when she told him that she'd also been dating another guy and the two of them had decided to date exclusively. Just like that, their relationship was over.

Ty had broken up with at least 20 girls over the years. But here was Natalie dumping him, only the third girl to ever do that. Ty hated rejection and longed for the control he usually had in these situations.

*I need to be more careful when I talk about work,* he thought. *She probably stopped dating me because I was too much of a complainer. I won't make that mistake again.*

# Chapter 20
## *Spring Break in Beijing*

"That dinner was amazing," said Anthony. "You're such a great cook."

Olivia smiled. "It wasn't anything special. You're just easy to please. And I like that about you. So, what time do you leave on your spring break trip?"

"Our flight leaves pretty early in the morning. I can't remember exactly when. And we get back really late in the evening the following Monday. Luckily, I've only got two classes on Monday. My friends are going to take notes for me, so I won't miss anything."

"Nice. It's three of you going, right? You, Ben, and Jared?"

"Yep," said Anthony. "Jared's dad works for an airline and got us buddy passes. Believe it or not, I can go to Beijing and back for just $250. I can't wait to explore Asia a bit."

"I'd love to go sometime," she said. "A friend of mine went last year. She said it's a fascinating place, but the pollution is horrible."

"Yeah, so I've heard. But smog or no smog, we're super excited to see the Great Wall, the Forbidden City, the Temple of Heaven, the Summer Olympic sites, the Ming tombs, Tiananmen Square, and whatever other places we come across."

"It sounds fascinating. Take lots of pictures."

"Of course. And I'll try to call or text every day. It could be tricky, because the time zones are so different. I promise to never call you at 3:00 a.m. your time," he said.

"You're a dear," said Olivia with a smile. "Anyhow, don't feel like you need to talk to me every day. I know you'll be busy and, like you said, the different time zones might make it hard to find a good time. You can tell me everything once you get back."

"It's strange, but I already miss you," said Anthony.

"I feel the same way," agreed Olivia. "By the way, make sure you don't accidently leave your backpack somewhere. I hear that a lot of really smart people do that on trips. Unless you have your own personal Good Samaritan, it can really ruin your plans."

As Anthony and Olivia shared a long hug and longer goodbye kiss, they had no idea how much things would change before he returned from China.

# Chapter 21
## *Very, Very Sorry*

On the same Monday that Anthony began his eight-day trip to Beijing, Ty bought a dozen yellow roses in a vase with a yellow ribbon tied around it. He almost opted for the red roses but remembered at the last minute that yellow roses were Olivia's favorite. He attached a card to the vase and rang her doorbell. He'd left his car around the corner, so he was well out of sight by the time she opened the door.

Thinking that Anthony had arranged for the flower delivery, Olivia smiled and read the card.

*Dear Olivia, I'm very, very sorry about how I handled things when I left Provo. Please forgive me. Would you have dinner with me tomorrow night? I really miss you. Love, Ty.*

Stunned, Olivia sat down on the porch steps. Her mind raced.

*He disappears without a word and now, eight months later, he wants to have dinner with me. Why? What changed?*

She wasn't sure she could trust Ty, but the note and flowers made her feel wanted. And it always feels wonderful to be wanted.

The selfish way Ty ended their relationship had left her feeling humiliated and vulnerable. However, the note he'd just delivered was humble and apologetic.

Olivia was a woman divided. Part of her wanted nothing to do with Ty. After all, she knew he was capable of unkindness. Plus, she wasn't even sure that she could trust him. She stared at the roses. *Why would I ever in a million years think of dating Ty again?*

But another part of Olivia yearned for closure. The fact that she still sometimes thought about Ty proved that she hadn't completely purged him from her life. If she could spend time with him again, even if it were just a few dates, she might be able to get the clarity and closure necessary to dedicate her heart to Anthony.

She knew that people are capable of mighty changes. Ty could now be a better version of himself. More thoughtful. More sincere. Ever since Olivia was a young girl, she had always been quick to forgive others. Her parents felt that her willingness to freely forgive was one of her most endearing spiritual gifts.

*The scriptures are filled with stories of people who dramatically changed for the better.* She decided that she wouldn't respond to Ty until the following morning. She needed time to reflect on this surprising turn of events.

She also felt that it would be good for him to have to wait for an answer. She didn't want to come across too eager. After all he'd put her through, she didn't want to make things too easy for him.

Later that evening, Olivia and her mom were discussing things in the kitchen when her dad arrived home.

"Are you going to start dating that guy again?" he asked.

"I never thought he'd ask me out again, so I haven't made a final decision yet. You've told me many times that we miss 100% of the shots we don't take."

Her dad nodded in agreement. "That's true, but I also believe in the saying, 'Once burned, twice cautious.' It still bothers me that Ty treated you so poorly."

"It still bothers me, too," she said.

Her mom then asked, "If you start dating Ty, will you end things with Anthony?"

"No. I definitely want to keep dating Anthony. Eventually, I'll have to choose one or the other, assuming they both stay interested in me. I feel like getting closure with Ty might be an important part of strengthening my relationship with Anthony."

"Dating two guys will be tricky," her dad said. "It'd be one thing if you were in the early stages of a relationship, but you dated Ty for several months and now you've dated Anthony exclusively for the last two months. I doubt they'll want to be part of a dating triangle. You'll have to choose one or the other, and sooner than later."

"I see what you're saying," agreed Olivia.

"Think of it from Anthony's point of view," her dad continued. "He'll be deeply hurt if all of a sudden you start going out with someone else. In order to spend time with Ty, you'll probably have to see Anthony less often. There are only so many days and hours in a week."

Her mom then asked, "Do you think Ty and Anthony are alike?"

"They're both smart, fun, and hardworking. Anthony is not as classically good-looking as Ty, but almost no one is. I really like the way Anthony smiles with his eyes. He's also kind and thoughtful."

"How a person looks on the outside plays an important role in physical attraction," her mom said. "But over time, inner qualities like Anthony's can add a lot of fuel to the romantic fire."

On Tuesday morning, Anthony called Olivia from Beijing. She didn't mention to him that she was thinking of having dinner with her former boyfriend that evening.

Olivia felt uncomfortable and somewhat disloyal about the idea of dating Ty again, but neither she nor Anthony had ever specifically said, "Let's only date each other." What she wanted most was closure. Either she'd rekindle things with Ty, which seemed unlikely, or she would confirm that Ty was unworthy of her time and attention.

Anthony deserved her full attention, and this seemed like the only way to make that happen. With him gone for the rest of the week, the timing seemed ideal.

An hour later, Olivia was about to send a text to Ty inviting him to dinner when a wave of doubt passed over her. He'd broken her heart before. She thought of the saying, "Hurt me once, shame on you. Hurt me twice, shame on me."

But she was reassured by the knowledge that people can change. If Ty really was a better person and wanted to treat her right, she owed it to herself to spend a little time with him.

There was one last concern that Olivia had to resolve. What would Anthony think? She worried all morning. She wasn't certain, but she felt that Anthony would keep dating her, even if she were also dating Ty at the same time. *Anthony has always been very kind and patient,* she thought.

Olivia took a deep breath. She then invited Ty to dinner. She told him that her parents would be gone, so it would be just the two of them.

"Sounds great," Ty quickly responded. "I'll see you at 7:00."

# Chapter 22
## *Return of the Prodigal Boyfriend*

Olivia felt both excited and nervous as she watched Ty walk toward her home. She noticed a girl watching him from the other side of the street. When she'd dated Ty in Provo, she sometimes felt vulnerable when she saw other girls admiring him. Other times, she felt proud.

Before he arrived, she'd thought a lot about what to say to him. Because of his past behavior, she was hesitant to start dating again. He would need to prove himself before she'd even think about opening her heart to him.

She smiled only slightly as she opened the door. It was the first time she'd seen Ty in eight months. *He's even more beautiful than I remembered, and he still has that adorable smile.*

They exchanged a hug. She had expected it to be awkward but found it quite comfortable.

"Hi, Ty. It's good to see you again."

"Great to see you, too!"

"The lasagna needs 10 more minutes," said Olivia. "Let's hang out in the living room until it's ready."

As soon as they sat down, Olivia thanked Ty for the roses. She had placed them on the table where they'd be having dinner together.

Just a few moments later, she received a call from her Grandma Angela, who had left a prescription at Olivia's home earlier that day. Angela wasn't feeling well and asked Olivia to please bring her the medicine right away.

"I'm sorry, but I need to take some medication to my grandma. I'll be back in 15 minutes. Do you mind staying here and taking out the lasagna when the buzzer goes off?"

"No problem," he said.

Ty was a naturally curious soul, so after Olivia left, he decided to do some exploring. His first stop was her parents' bedroom. When he felt an urge to check out their medicine cabinet in the adjoining bathroom, a twinge of guilt prompted him to stop. He started to walk away, but his curiosity ultimately got the best of him. He entered the bathroom and found two prescription bottles in the cabinet. Ty recognized the names of both medicines. *Very interesting*, he thought.

He next went looking for Olivia's room. Ty was rather unorganized, like his dad, but wanted to marry a well-organized woman, like his mom. He smiled when he entered her immaculate bedroom.

He soon noticed a photo of Olivia with her brothers, parents, and deceased sister, Bella. Bella's hair was longer and lighter in color than Olivia's, but their facial features were virtually identical. They looked about 20 years old. As he gazed at the photo, Ty felt compassion for Olivia and her family.

In Olivia's bathroom, he found a sparkling sink, a spotless mirror, and one prescription bottle. He didn't recognize her medication, so he typed its name into his phone for future research.

Walking back into her bedroom, he noticed a leather-bound book on the desk. He grinned when he saw the word "Journal" imprinted on the cover.

*This could be a gold mine*, he thought. But then he waivered. *I shouldn't be reading her journal. That's a major invasion of privacy.*

Ty wrestled with his decision for at least a full minute. He then opened Olivia's journal and began to read. He was impressed that she wrote in her journal every day. He had reviewed four pages of the journal without seeing any mention of his name when the oven buzzer sounded. He hurried to the kitchen and took out the lasagna. He then rushed back to her room.

Moments later, his phone rang. "Did you remember to take out the lasagna?"

"Sure did, and it smells wonderful. How's your grandma doing?"

"She's okay," said Olivia. "But she needs a little more help. I might be a bit longer than I thought."

"Take all of the time you need. I'm just reading a book I had in my car."

After they finished their call, Ty quickly returned to examining the journal. He decided to focus on her most recent entries, starting with what Olivia had written that very morning:

*Last night I had a great talk with Grandma Angela. She told me that if I start dating Ty again, I shouldn't ignore warning signs just because he's the best-*

*looking guy I've ever dated. She said the high divorce rate in Hollywood is a powerful reminder that there is much more to a happy marriage than just physical attraction. She told me that kindness is the foundation of a loving marriage and she thinks that Ty broke up with me in a way that showed a lack of kindness. She also said that he acted like a coward when he left without saying goodbye.*

It greatly annoyed Ty that Grandma Angela would describe him as a coward who lacked kindness, but he loved Olivia's comment that he was the best-looking guy around. He then read the last paragraph of her journal entry.

*If Ty wants to date me again, I hope he'll show more of a personal interest in me and in my ideas. He was a pretty good listener when we dated in Provo, but Anthony is a GREAT listener. Anthony asks me a lot of thoughtful questions. I can always tell he cares what I think.*

Ty made a mental note to listen better and to ask better questions. He quickly returned to the living room and sat down on the sofa less than five seconds before Olivia walked through the front door.

*Wow. That was too close.* He realized that it would've been incredibly hard to explain why he was in her bedroom if she had found him there.

During dinner, they talked about their jobs, families, and wards. Their conversation went better than she would have expected. He let her do most of the talking and asked dozens of thoughtful questions.

Not only that, but Ty also offered to help clean up. Once the dishes were all in the dishwasher and the rest of the meal had been put away, they sat by each other on a sofa in the living room. As she looked into his dazzling blue eyes, he chose his words carefully.

"I'm so sorry about the awful way I ended our relationship," he said with as much contrition as he could muster. "I was selfish and insensitive. I hope you can forgive me one day, but I realize it'll take time. When I was dating you, I was happy. I haven't been as happy since. It's that simple. I miss you and I really want to start dating again."

She said nothing, so he continued talking. "You are smart and happy and fun. You're the kindest and most beautiful girl I've ever dated."

Her voice was trembled, and tears filled her eyes. "I was devastated when you disappeared. I'll never understand how you could do that to me. If I started to date you, I'd worry that you'd just disappear again. For a while now, I've been dating a wonderful guy named Anthony. I know he'd never treat me like that."

"I know I hurt you, but I want to earn back your trust."

Olivia was silent for what seemed to Ty a very long time. Finally, she said, "I'd be willing to date you again, but only one date at a time. If we both feel good about our next date, then we could go on another one. I want to take things slowly."

"That's a good idea. Do you want to go on a hike tomorrow night, then we can grab some gelato? I know you love gelato."

"That sounds good."

On Thursday afternoon, they both left work early so they could hike up Prospector's Canyon. There wasn't a single cloud in the azure sky.

The following night, Olivia told him she was going out to dinner with some high school friends. She felt good about taking a one-day break from dating Ty. She didn't want to rush things.

On Saturday, they went to a play on campus called My Imperfectly Happy Life. Ty laughed a lot during the performance. Olivia had always liked the sound of his joyful, easy laugh.

Although the play was funny, it also explored serious themes. The main character, a girl in her late 20s, was a perfectionist who focused so much on minor things that she drove others away.

Halfway through the story, an optimistic new boyfriend with an easy-going sense of humor emerged on the scene. He gradually helped the main character to relax and enjoy her good, but imperfect, life.

As they walked to Ty's car, Olivia began to hum a traditional Italian song. "I've missed your music," Ty said. "I remember how nice it was when you'd sing to me in Provo."

He then apologized once more for hurting her.

"I know it might take a long time, but I hope one day you'll forgive me for the way I ended things. I'm sorry I handled everything so badly and hurt your feelings."

Olivia surprised Ty, and herself, when she put her hand on his arm and said, "I forgive you."

Both her heart and his felt happier after she'd said those three healing words.

"Thank you," he said. "I never thought you'd be able to forgive me so soon."

Later that night, Olivia felt doubt come over her once more. Ty was charming and charismatic, but could he be trusted? That was the question she needed answered.

# Chapter 23
## *Thee Lift Me, and Me Lift Thee*

Ty and Olivia hurried to the Institute building, hoping they weren't too late to find a good seat. The speaker was Brother Fawson, a member of the faculty. He started his remarks by sharing the true story of Tilly Smith.

"On December 26, 2004, a massive earthquake struck the Indian Ocean," Brother Fawson said. "The earthquake, and the many tsunamis it triggered, killed more than 230,000 people. It was one of the deadliest natural disasters in recorded history.

"Two weeks before that day of destruction, a 10-year-old English girl named Tilly Smith was listening to her teacher give a geography lesson. The teacher told the students that there are two warning signs of an impending tsunami: water receding from the shoreline and frothing bubbles on the surface of the water.

"That tragic day began calmly. Tilly was playing on a beach in Thailand with her parents and her younger sister when the tide suddenly rushed out. The surface of the sea then began to bubble. Tilly urgently told her parents that they had to get everyone off the beach because a tsunami was coming.

"At first, her parents felt that Tilly was overreacting. But Tilly wouldn't take no for an answer. She adamantly insisted that a tsunami was coming soon. She told her parents that she'd been taught the signs of a tsunami. Her parents then did something that saved their lives, as well as the lives of many others. They listened to their 10-year old daughter and alerted the hotel staff.

"The beach was quickly evacuated. A short time later, an enormous wave struck. It was so powerful that it would've killed anyone who had remained on the beach. That day, Tilly saved the lives of almost 100 people, including her family.

"She received many honors for her heroic actions. She was invited to the United Nations to receive a special award. Tilly's teacher back in England also was honored for teaching her the warning signs of a tsunami.

"To bless others, we need knowledge about how to bless them. But we also need to act on our knowledge. That's exactly what Tilly Smith did."

Brother Fawson then transitioned to a different topic. "Let's talk for a few minutes about love. It's the most beautiful word in the English language, after all. But there's another important word that should go hand-in-hand with love: wisdom. I like to compare love to the engine in a car. It gives the car power, but that power needs to be carefully controlled. So, what helps to control the engine's power? The brakes, the gas pedal, and the steering wheel.

"If you're dating, don't just look for a person who is loving. Look for a person who is wise. Love and wisdom are like two sides of the same coin. It's like one hand washing the other. Wisdom guides and protects love."

Brother Fawson concluded his talk by recounting a story from the 12th century. "This story might be true, or it might just be a legend, but either way it's inspiring."

*Many centuries ago, a large castle in Germany was under siege. A powerful king led the army that surrounded the castle. The king gave the women in the castle permission to leave without being harmed but said the men could not leave.*

*The army's intent was to attack the men in the castle. The women living in the castle asked if they could take with them everything that they could carry on their backs. The king agreed.*

*The day came for the women to leave the castle. As they left, each woman was carrying her husband on her back. The king was so impressed with the loyalty of the wives that he allowed them to leave with their husbands. The castle is still called the Castle of the Loyal Wives.*

As they left the fireside that evening, Ty said to Olivia, "Would you mind putting me on your back and carrying me to the car? I'm really tired."

She laughed out loud. Ty then took her in his arms and carried her the rest of the way.

"Will you date me exclusively for one month?" he asked. "I came so close to proposing to you in Provo. If we date only each other for the next month, I'm confident we'll either get engaged, or I'll let you move on."

"I would love to get that kind of closure," replied Olivia. "I'll think about it."

Shortly after Olivia returned from the fireside, she received a call from Anthony. It was still Sunday in Savona Springs, but it was Monday in Beijing.

"I've had a change of plans," said Anthony. "Ben got really sick. He's in the hospital and the doctors say he won't be able to travel for another few days. Jared has to get back home for work, so I'm going to stay with Ben. I'm going to email my professors, so hopefully it won't be a big deal to miss more school. For me, the biggest problem is that I want to be back with you. I've really missed you."

"I've really missed you, too," she said. "And I'm sorry about Ben. Hope he's okay!"

After their call ended, Anthony couldn't escape the feeling that things had changed. Olivia was still warm and friendly, but he sensed that something was off.

As Olivia and Ty looked over the dinner menu, she asked him if he was enjoying his work as an attorney.

"It's a great firm and I really like the people I work with." He intentionally sanitized his answer, because he didn't want her to think he was a complainer.

"Glad your job is working out so well," she replied. "I've only eaten here at Mario's once before, by the way. I know their spaghetti is supposed to be amazing, but what do you recommend?"

"Since you love Italian food, I'd recommend the shrimp pasta parmesan. That's what I'm having. It's amazing."

Olivia wasn't usually a fan of seafood and hadn't eaten any for many years, but she loved pasta and parmesan cheese. She decided to be adventuresome and follow Ty's recommendation.

When the main dish arrived, she took a few bites of shrimp and said, "It's delicious." After a few more bites, she could feel her throat beginning to constrict. Ty saw panic in her eyes. She was struggling to breathe.

He stood up and yelled, "We need a doctor!"

A woman hurried across the room. "I'm a doctor. I think your friend is having an allergic reaction."

She asked a waiter, "Do you have an EpiPen in the kitchen?"

"I think so. I'll go grab it!" He ran into the kitchen, but after a full minute, he still hadn't returned with an EpiPen.

"Call an ambulance!" the doctor said to Ty. "She's not getting enough air."

Ty was just hanging up with emergency dispatch when the waiter finally emerged from the kitchen. He handed an EpiPen to the doctor, who then swiftly stuck it into Olivia's thigh. The adrenaline soon began doing its work and her throat became less constricted.

After Olivia was examined at the hospital, a doctor told Ty, "She's going to be fine, but we want to keep her here for two or three hours, just to be sure. Many food allergies start in childhood, but seafood allergies can be sneaky. They sometimes start a lot later in life."

Olivia called her mom and explained what had happened. "I feel totally fine now, but they want me to stay for a couple more hours."

Her mom wanted to come straight to the hospital, but she was busy helping her own dad, who was having a tough night. She took comfort in the fact that Olivia seemed happy and relaxed.

"Please stay there with Grandpa," Olivia said. "I feel fine, and Ty offered to stay here at the hospital with me until I'm released. It won't be long."

"Alright," her mom said reluctantly. "But call me right away if you have any problems. And pass on my thanks to Ty for staying with you!"

Just as the doctors had predicted, Olivia was released two hours later. As Ty walked her up the sidewalk toward her house, she asked him if he'd like to come in for a bit.

"I think you should get some rest," he replied.

"You're probably right. Do you want to come to dinner here tomorrow night? And we could maybe go to a movie?"

He smiled. "Sounds great. I'm so glad everything turned out okay tonight."

"Thanks for taking such good care of me," said Olivia. "It meant a lot. Also, I talked to Anthony last night. One of his friends is in a hospital, so he won't be able to fly back until Thursday afternoon."

Ty tried his best to act concerned by the news, but she could see the excited look in his eyes.

Before she went to sleep, Olivia revisited the tender way Ty had supported her. *Ty has somehow become a sweeter version of himself,* she thought. *And I don't necessarily know why. Most people don't seem to change much, but I'm glad he has.*

When Ty came over for dinner the following night, they both still seemed to be riding high from their bonding experience in the hospital.

After finishing the meal, they quickly tossed the dishes in the sink so they could make it to the theater in time for the movie.

The movie, an action thriller that Ty chose, turned out to be a disappointment. However, they were both still in good spirits as they drove home. Ty turned to Olivia and said, "I asked you to think about dating me exclusively. Now that you've had some time, what do you think?"

"I've been giving it a lot of thought, but I still don't know."

Sensing that she didn't want to sever things with Anthony, Ty decided to make a bold move. He thought that the timing was appropriate because of all the support he'd shown her throughout the allergic reaction incident.

"Let's just try it for a month," he said in a soft tone. "I think you might lose both of us if you try to date me and Anthony at the same time. People don't like to be juggled. Just choose one of us to date for the next month. If that doesn't work, then you can move on."

*Does he really prefer not dating me at all if he can't have me to himself?* she wondered.

Ty then added one more twist. "The receptionist at our firm has been showing a lot of interest in me. I'd rather date you, but I guess I could spend more time with her if you decide you still want to explore things with Anthony."

Olivia was silent. Ty's comment about the receptionist at his office made her feel vulnerable and slightly manipulated. She also remembered her dad saying it could be tricky if she tried to date Anthony and Ty at the same time.

"I need to think about this more, but I'll give you an answer soon."

On Wednesday, they went for a run in Veteran's Park. The weather was uncommonly hot, so both of them petered out faster than they'd planned. Drenched in sweat, they made their way back to Ty's car.

"Have you made up your mind?" Ty asked.

She told him again that she wasn't ready to make a final decision.

He smiled and said, "That's fine. I don't want to rush you."

Olivia had trouble going to sleep that night. Her mind was working overtime.

*How can I choose between two people I care for in such different ways? It's not like looking at two apples and deciding which one is better. Ty and Anthony are both great guys, but they couldn't be more unlike each other. They have different personalities and different goals.*

When the alarm clock jolted her awake, Olivia realized she'd finally been able to drift off to sleep. Her restless night had unfortunately left her groggy and sluggish. Nonetheless, she'd made her agonizing decision.

Anthony had returned from China. Later that evening, he was coming to dinner.

# Chapter 24
## *Alone*

Anthony was ecstatic as he drove to Olivia's house. His extended time in China had been full of adventures he couldn't wait to tell her about. Most of all, her absence had made his heart grow even fonder.

He stopped at the florist on Main Street and bought a dozen yellow roses. As his car approached her neighborhood, he thought about proposing to her that very night, right after dinner. He felt ready, but she had told him several times that she didn't want to rush things. Perhaps it would be best for him to wait at least a month or two.

Because she'd been badly burned once, Olivia seemed to be twice as cautious.

On his long flight back to California, Anthony had pictured the two of them walking together through the journey of life as husband and wife, hand-in-hand, committed to loving each other in times of joy and sorrow.

Pulling into her driveway, his heart rate increased. It had been 12 days since he'd seen Olivia. He'd spoken to her most days while he was in China, but sometimes the different times zones had prevented them from connecting.

Olivia greeted him at the door with a hug and a kiss. She thanked him for the beautiful roses. But Anthony immediately sensed that something was wrong. His heart sank as he stepped into the house that suddenly felt a bit less inviting.

She had prepared a great meal, but their dinner conversation didn't flow as smoothly as in the past. One of the things he loved about Olivia had always been her warm personality and ability to put people at ease, but she seemed worried and distracted.

After they finished eating, they sat on the sofa.

"There's something I need to tell you," she said gently.

Sadness descended on her like fog rolling in from the sea. She shook her head slightly as she said to Anthony, "I'm sorry. This is really, really hard."

She had rehearsed what she would say but knew that he'd feel hurt and rejected no matter how she explained it. She had chosen Ty over Anthony for the next month. Maybe forever.

It had been the hardest decision of her life. But it came down to getting closure from Ty so that she could finally heal completely from the wounds he'd dealt her. Maybe she'd quickly get clarity and decide to move on from Ty, or perhaps their relationship would grow into something beautiful. She needed to know either way. And she owed it to Anthony to find out, so that she could fully commit to him if she were to choose him in the end. She could only hope he would still be waiting for her.

Anthony shifted his body and turned his head so that he was looking directly into her beautiful eyes. She gently took hold of his hands. Her hands were cold, and her chin had started to tremble slightly. There was no easy way to deliver the bad news, so Olivia got right to the point.

"As I told you before, I dated a guy in Provo for several months and we came close to getting engaged. His name is Ty. He's now living here, and he contacted me out of the blue the same day you left on your trip. I went out with him often while you were gone."

The word "often" was an understatement. They'd been together for 10 of the last 11 days.

This conversation came as a shock to Anthony. Because the two of them had spent so much time together over the last two months, and because she'd told him so many times that she loved him, he had assumed that they were dating exclusively.

He now realized that he'd assumed too much.

Olivia drew a deep breath. "I love you, Anthony," she said. "There is so much about you that I admire. But I also care for Ty, and I need to find out if there's still something there between us."

Tears filled her eyes. "This has been an incredibly hard decision for me, but I really feel like I should focus on Ty for a month. We'll either be engaged, or we'll be ready to move on. I just need that closure. There's a good chance that we won't get engaged. We broke up once before, after all. If I don't get engaged to him, I'd absolutely love to start dating you again."

Anthony wasn't ready to give up. "Have you forgotten that Ty is the same guy who left you without even saying goodbye? Why would you want to date someone like that again?"

She paused, then said, "People can change. I think Ty has changed. He's more thoughtful and kind than he was before."

Anthony tried a different approach. "So, does this mean you won't be coming with me to the *Giant of the City* gala next week? You accepted my invitation over a month ago."

"I'm sorry, but I made a commitment to Ty that I'd date only him."

"But you made a commitment to me first. Just tell Ty you promised a long time ago that you'd go with me. I've always felt you were a person who kept your promises. One date isn't going to make a difference."

"I'll give Ty a call right now," she replied. "I think he might be willing to let me go."

She then went to another room in the house to make the call. After a few minutes, she returned. "Sorry, but I won't be able to go with you. I'm sure you'll find a great date."

As she looked into his eyes, she saw his crushing disappointment. Tears began to run down her cheeks. "I'm so sorry. I don't know what else to say except that I hope you'll respect my decision."

They both sat in silence as the old clock in the hallway rhythmically ticked and hummed.

Finally, Anthony spoke. "The most wonderful thing about you is the way you love others. No other girl has ever made me feel so happy, and so loved. But now that you've chosen Ty, it's clear you love him more than you love me. It seems like it's probably time for me to move on."

"I really do care for both of you, but I can't date you at the same time. I had to make a choice."

"And you made your choice," Anthony said. His voice had become softer in defeat. "Choosing Ty shows me where your heart is, Olivia. It's that simple. I think I should go now."

"Will you date me again if things don't work out with me and Ty?" Olivia asked.

Anthony was quiet. He then said, "It's not the same now that you've chosen him. I think we should go our separate ways, whether or not it works out between you two. Thank you for all the great memories. You're the kindest person I've ever met, and I love you."

"I love you, too," she said. "I love you so much."

They then gave each other the longest hug they'd ever shared.

As Anthony walked away from Olivia's home, she noticed that his head was held high and his shoulders were square. She'd seen the pain in his eyes. She was sure his heart was bruised and battered, yet he walked away like a man full of hope and confidence. Like a man who was not coming back.

She now realized that she'd misjudged Anthony. Yes, he was kind. But he was also stronger and more decisive than she thought. He had no intention of waiting around to see if things were going to work out with her and Ty. She had made her choice and he was ready to move on, even though he knew he'd deeply miss being with her.

She watched Anthony's taillights fade into the night, then sat down on the sofa, put her head in her hands, and started to weep. She kept thinking about something Anthony had said. *I've always felt you were a person who kept your promises.*

She waited an hour before calling Ty, telling him she could commit to dating him for the next month. He was ecstatic.

Olivia felt no such excitement. She was deeply worried that she'd lost Anthony for good, even if things did not work out with Ty. She had treated Anthony as her back-up plan, but he had no interest in fulfilling that role.

Anthony suddenly felt a pain in his chest. For a moment he thought that he might be having a heart attack, and he considered pulling over to the side of the road. The pain soon went away, but the sadness and loneliness lingered on. It had all happened so quickly and unexpectedly, like a bolt of lightning coming down from a clear sky.

When he'd rung Olivia's doorbell earlier that evening, he thought he was coming back to a joyful "welcome home" dinner with the girl he loved. Instead, he'd been blindsided.

He felt abandoned. Shipwrecked. Rejected. Worst of all, he felt alone.

When he arrived at his mom's house, all was quiet. She'd flown to Colorado to visit her sister.

*Maybe it was a mistake to go to China for such a long time*, he thought. *Out of sight, out of mind.*

He sat down at the table and stared at the drips slowly forming on the kitchen faucet. He hoped he'd done the right thing when he told Olivia that he was moving on rather than waiting to see how things turned out.

That night he slept for less than three hours. When he woke the following morning, he felt a deep and consuming desire to be with Olivia. He craved the gentleness in her voice and her radiant smile, but it was not to be. The heartbreaking truth was that Olivia had chosen Ty.

Even though Anthony knew he'd greatly miss Olivia, he refused to feel sorry for himself. And he refused to give up hope that he would someday find another girl as amazing as Olivia.

# Chapter 25
## *As Silent as a Sphinx*

The following morning, Ty arrived at Parks & Lane in excellent spirits. His future was illuminating in ways he'd never imagined, and the good news continued to roll in. Millicent Fenwick had called to tell him that he was one of just three remaining finalists in the search for the face of the ad campaign.

As he walked through the firm's reception area on his way to lunch, Ty stopped for a moment to chat with Allison, the firm's tall and sunny receptionist.

"Are you still enjoying things here?" he asked.

"Yeah, everyone's super nice. But I miss Alaska. I'm probably going to go back there for a couple weeks this summer."

Ty smiled. "Sounds fun. I've always wanted to go Alaska. Anyhow, have a good day!"

"You too," Allison said.

*She's really cute,* he thought.

At that moment, Olivia's Grandpa, Ezra Harris, entered the reception area.

"Hi, Ty, how are you doing?" Ezra asked.

Ty was surprised that Ezra remembered his name. "I'm fine, Mr. Harris. How are you doing?"

"I'm well, thank you."

Ty was planning to meet a friend for lunch, but lingered in the reception area, pretending to check his phone.

He soon overheard Ezra say to Allison, "I have an appointment with Mr. Parks. I don't think it should take long. I just need to sign off on yet another revision to my will."

Ty's stomach started to churn. *Did Ezra's new will cut back Olivia's inheritance? If so, how deep was the cut? Could she be totally out of the will?*

Fletcher arrived in the reception area and greeted Ezra. Ty watched the two men walk down the hall and enter Fletcher's office. He yearned to be a fly on the wall. He'd actually once seen a movie in which a man had the ability to turn into a fly that could spy on others. But since Ty had no such powers, he grudgingly left the office.

"Ezra, I want to confirm all the changes before you sign this updated will," Fletcher said. "You told me your daughter Mary will now get your home, all of your personal property, and the first $2.5 million of cash in your estate rather than the first $3 million. You also told me your grandchildren will still receive $1 million each. The additional $500,000 will be divided equally between the two charities named in your will. If all those amendments sound correct, we can go ahead and sign your will."

"I feel good about these changes," Ezra said. "Mary loves where she lives and has no intention of ever moving. Since she doesn't want to build or buy a new house, it makes sense for me to give more of the money to charity."

Ezra took a sip of water, then continued. "I know there is some risk in giving $1 million to grandchildren who are only in their 20s, but life is full of risks and my grandchildren are quite responsible. It's thrilling for me to consider the great things they will do in life. And if this inheritance can aid them in their pursuits, that's all the better."

Later that afternoon, Ty was summoned to Fletcher's office. "Here's a short research project for you," said Fletcher, handing him a one-page document. "I'm flying to Denver tonight and I'll be gone for two or three days."

"I'll have it ready before you get back," Ty said pleasantly, even though he was frustrated that his heavy workload had just become even heavier. He'd learned early on that older attorneys often underestimate how long it takes a younger attorney to finish things like research projects.

As Ty was leaving, Fletcher's secretary entered the office. "Betsy, the lock on my door is broken. Would you please make sure it gets fixed tomorrow?"

"Will do," she said.

That evening, Olivia and Ty went to dinner at a new Mexican restaurant. The food was excellent, but a little too spicy for her taste.

"You seem distracted tonight," she said.

She was right. Ty was distracted. He was thinking about Ezra's revised will and wondering if Olivia was still in it.

"I'm sorry," he replied. "I'm dealing with a challenging situation at work, but that's enough about me."

He then proceeded to ask her questions about her work at The Melby Foundation. After dinner, they went to a movie.

Ty arrived at his office early the following morning. He walked through the entire building to make sure the coast was clear. Then he entered Fletcher's office through the unlocked door.

As he navigated the darkened room, Ty noticed a signed SSU football on the desk. He knew that Fletcher was a major booster for the school. He then saw three stacks of documents. After searching through the first two stacks without finding anything of interest, he struck gold in the third stack. It contained a folder with the words "Ezra Harris - Revised Will" written on the tab.

Ty confirmed that the revised will had been signed the day before. On the second page of the will, he found the section that he desperately wanted to review. It was entitled, "Gifts to My Daughter and My Grandchildren." Ty took a deep breath as he started to read.

*Gifts to My Daughter and to My Grandchildren. I leave my only child, Mary, my home, all of my personal property, and cash in the amount of $2,500,000. After the gift to Mary, I leave to each of my three grandchildren — Jonah Michaels, Olivia Michaels, and Derek Michaels — cash in the amount of $1,000,000 each.*

"Olivia still gets a million!" he exclaimed, pumping his fist in the air. His sense of relief was enormous. As an act of celebration, he picked up the SSU football and threw it in the air. The ball bounced off the ceiling and landed on the expensive wool carpet that covered the office floor.

"Nice throw," someone said in a deep, resonant voice that sounded a lot like the actor Morgan Freeman.

As Ty turned toward the direction of the voice, his heart turned to ice.

Fletcher was silently standing by the door to his office, which was now wide open. Ty's mind went blank. He was as silent as a sphinx.

"I guess you didn't know I'm a very early riser," Fletcher said.

Ty was still speechless. Finally, he managed to mutter, "I can explain this."

"I doubt it." Fletcher did not invite him to sit down, so he gave his explanation standing up.

100

"I came into work early today because I couldn't find my phone. I searched my apartment last night, then searched my office this morning. When I didn't find my phone, I started checking other offices, including yours, to see if someone picked up my phone by mistake. As you know, many of us have phones that look alike."

Ty was having trouble forming his words because his mouth was so dry.

Fletcher took out his phone and dialed a number. Ty's phone began ringing in his suit coat pocket. "I think you just found your missing phone. Next time, look in your pocket before breaking into my office."

Fletcher then moved over to his desk. "I see that Ezra's revised will is here on my desk, opened to the exact page that shows how much his grandchildren will inherit."

Ty didn't know what to say, so he said nothing.

"You snuck into my office to read Ezra's revised will, even after I clearly told you that you could have nothing more to do this. You do remember me telling you that, don't you?"

Ty thought about lying, but instead told the truth. "Yes, I remember."

"Do you remember me stopping by your office to tell you a second time that you could not have anything more to do with this will?"

"Yes," said Ty. "I remember and I'm very sorry. I promise you that nothing like this will ever happen again. May I leave now?"

Fletcher erupted.

"No, you can't leave now!" This was the first time Fletcher had ever yelled at Ty. Luckily, it was early in the morning so no one else was in the office to hear the explosion.

"You lied to me! You looked me in the face and promised me you'd have nothing more to do with Ezra's will, then you broke into my office and read it. You did exactly what you told me you wouldn't do. I can't trust you anymore!"

"I'm sorry. I promise it won't happen again. May I go back to my office?"

"Yes, go back to your office. And I want you back here in my office tomorrow morning. My trip to Denver has been cancelled. If I had to make a decision right now, I'd fire you. But I'm not going to make a final decision until tomorrow. I'll take a day to think about it."

Ty once again apologized. He also told Fletcher that he was on his own financially, had extensive student debt, and that his dad had serious medical problems. In short, he really, really needed this job.

Ty then returned to his office, but he was useless for the rest of the day.

*I can't believe Fletcher would fire me over this,* he thought. *No one got hurt. No one lost any money. I looked at the will, but I didn't change it at all.*

Ty then realized that Olivia might not marry him if Parks & Lane fired him. *I could lose both my job and Olivia,* he thought in a moment of despair.

Fletcher had calmed down somewhat by the next morning, but he was still angry with Ty. "I know I should fire you, but I haven't made a final decision. I might decide later today, or I might decide next week. Just know that you're on borrowed time. One more screwup and you'll be on the street."

Ty then returned to his office. He felt like he was trapped in a bad dream. At any moment on any given day, Fletcher might come into his office and tell him to pack his things.

# Chapter 26
## *The Heart Has a Mind of Its Own*

Ty stopped by The Melby Foundation to give Olivia a box of chocolates. He smiled and said, "Thanks again for telling Anthony that you're all mine for the next month."

They exchanged a kiss, but Ty sensed that something might be bothering her. He noticed she had several large stacks of documents on her desk. *She seems to be really busy today.*

That afternoon, Anthony paid a surprise visit to Grandma Angela, who was visibly disappointed Olivia had chosen Ty over him.

"I might be wrong, but I feel you and Olivia will get back together," Angela said. "When Ty left Olivia, it was a crushing blow to her self-esteem. He shattered her confidence. His desire to date her again has made Olivia feel better about herself, and we all want to feel good about ourselves. It's like she turned a humiliating defeat into a great victory when she started dating Ty again. But after she has been with Ty for a while, I think she will realize that she loves you most. That's what I'm hoping for, anyway. Sometimes the heart has a mind of its own."

Anthony shook his head and said, "Olivia made her choice, so I need to move on. I've already asked a girl to dinner tomorrow night. She seems really nice."

Olivia awoke with a start. She had been in the middle of a disturbing dream. She'd broken up with Ty, or maybe he broke up with her. That specific detail wasn't clear, but one way or another, they were no longer dating each other.

All of a sudden, she found herself outside Anthony's door. She couldn't wait to tell him that her relationship with Ty was over. She rang his doorbell. When the door opened, a beautiful girl with a huge smile on her face was standing next to Anthony. They held hands and both looked ecstatic.

"Look at my gorgeous ring," the girl said to Olivia. "Anthony and I just got engaged."

Olivia was now alone.

*It's only a dream*, she said to herself after waking up. But she had a hard time falling back to sleep.

# Chapter 27
## *Two Girls in Purple Sweaters*

From 2003-2015, Martin Ziff had been the popular president of Savona Springs University. He often sat down with students in the cafeteria and joined in friendly conversation. He had planned to serve until he was 70, but at the age of 68, he died when he was hit by lightning while playing golf at the local country club.

To say President Ziff was unlucky would be an understatement. In the entire country, only 29 people died from lightning strikes that year. By contrast, more than 32,000 Americans lost their lives in car accidents during that same time period.

Although President Ziff was a brilliant man, he was also humble and friendly. There was not an arrogant bone in his body. His widow, Hazel Ziff, on the other hand, was a force to be reckoned with. She had supreme confidence in herself and in her opinions.

Hazel was always certain, but only sometimes right.

Two weeks earlier, on a sunny Friday, Mrs. Ziff was walking from her reserved parking space to the SSU Art Museum cafeteria where she was meeting a friend for lunch. Experiencing some shortness of breath, she sat down on a bench to rest for a moment. She placed her purse next to her on the bench.

A few minutes later, a girl with long brown hair and a purple sweater walked by the bench. The girl pointed and yelled, "The library is on fire!" As Mrs. Ziff looked toward the library, the girl snatched her purse and sprinted away. The purse contained $700 in cash, two credit cards, a checkbook, and a cell phone.

Mrs. Ziff went straight to the campus police station to file a report. Her purse, cell phone, and credit cards were soon found scattered under a bush on campus. The only thing missing was her $700 in cash.

Two weeks later, Mrs. Ziff was once again walking across campus. She'd been invited to a luncheon. As she approached the building where the event was being held, Mrs. Ziff saw a girl in a purple sweater. She quickly located a campus police officer, who recognized Mrs. Ziff as the wife of the former university president.

"That girl in a purple sweater stole $700 from my purse two weeks ago. I'm sure that's her. You need to arrest her right now."

Walking briskly, the officer caught up with the girl and said, "I need to ask you just a few questions." The girl seemed startled and concerned. A few moments later, Mrs. Ziff caught up with the officer and the girl. The girl heard Mrs. Ziff say angrily, "She's definitely the girl who stole my purse."

"What is your name?" the officer asked.

"Olivia Michaels."

"Are you an SSU student?"

"No. I'm just running an errand on campus."

"May I see some ID?" the officer asked.

As Olivia handed the officer her driver's license, her hands were shaking slightly. "Why are you asking for my ID?"

Mrs. Ziff interrupted. "You know you stole my purse."

"Are you sure she is the thief?" the officer asked.

"I'm positive."

"How positive?

"100% positive," Mrs. Ziff said.

"When was your purse stolen?" Olivia asked.

"You know exactly when it was stolen! It was stolen exactly two weeks ago today, on Friday around noon"

"Officer, two weeks ago on Friday at noon I was having lunch with a friend at Mamma's Place. I'll get him on the phone right now. His name is Anthony Hull."

"The Incredible Hull?"

"Yes, that's him."

Olivia called and explained the situation to Anthony.

"I'll be there in 15 minutes," he said.

When Anthony arrived, he gave the campus police a sworn statement that he was having lunch with Olivia at the time of the crime. No charges were brought against Olivia, even though Mrs. Ziff continued to insist that Olivia was the criminal who stole her purse.

As Anthony walked Olivia to her car, she said, "Thanks for coming so quickly. If it weren't for you, they'd have charged me based solely on Mrs. Ziff's testimony. I think she's off her rocker."

"Being overly confident is one of the main symptoms of pride," replied Anthony. "And from the little I know, Mrs. Ziff is a *very* proud woman."

She smiled at Anthony, realizing more than ever how much she'd missed being with him. "Once again, you've been my Good Samaritan. Thanks for watching out for me one more time."

"You're welcome," he said. He wanted to tell her how much he'd missed her but couldn't quite summon the courage or the words.

Olivia then gave him a long hug and whispered in his ear, "I've missed you."

"I've missed you, too."

He opened her car door, and she thanked him again for coming to help her. She waved goodbye as her car slowly pulled out of the parking lot. He smiled and waved back. Seeing Olivia again brought back wonderful memories of them dating, but it also was a reminder that she chose Ty.

Anthony sometimes felt that he was living in a cruel prison, locked away from the girl he loved, like the Count of Monte Cristo.

Although she knew Ty wouldn't be excited about it, Olivia baked a dozen coconut chocolate chip cookies and delivered them to Anthony's apartment. He wasn't home at the time, however, because he had a team function on campus. She left a thank-you note and the cookies with his roommate, along with a playfully stern warning that the cookies had better not vanish before Anthony returned.

An hour later, Anthony sent a text to Olivia. "Thanks so much for the amazing cookies. I've already eaten four!"

"Glad that you liked them," she texted back. "Thanks again for helping me."

When Olivia and Ty went to a movie later that night, she struggled to follow the plot. It wasn't that the story was convoluted. The problem was that she couldn't stop thinking about Anthony.

The Mrs. Ziff incident actually reminded Anthony of an undergraduate class he'd taken called The American Criminal Justice System. The professor was a former criminal law judge. During one class, a man walked into the room while the professor was teaching. As the professor continued talking, the man stood silently in front of the class. After a minute or so, he departed as mysteriously as he'd arrived.

A couple of days later, the professor projected photos of two men onto a large screen. The men did not resemble each other. The students were then asked to identify which of the men had come into the class earlier. Only 69% of the students picked the right man. Some of those who picked the wrong man felt strongly they'd chosen correctly.

The professor told the students that extensive research has confirmed that eyewitness testimony isn't always accurate. The human mind is not a flawless recorder. Sometimes we forget things quickly or confuse important details.

One week later, Mrs. Ziff received a call from the campus police. They had caught a girl trying to steal someone's purse. The girl eventually confessed to stealing several other purses on campus, including Mrs. Ziff's.

Even though the actual thief had confessed to the crime, Mrs. Ziff never apologized to Olivia for her false accusation.

*It's no wonder the Book of Mormon warns us so often about the dangers of pride,* Olivia thought as she recalled Mrs. Ziff's false accusation. *Pride prevents us from seeing things as they really are.*

# Chapter 28
## *Understanding Hearts*

As Olivia boarded her flight to Portland, she was pleasantly surprised to see the plane was not very full. She even found a completely empty row near the back.

Opening her copy of the Book of Mormon, she read chapter 12 of the Book of Mosiah. She was particularly struck by verse 27. It seemed new to her. It read: *Ye have not applied your hearts to understanding; therefore, ye have not been wise.*

She reflected on the way Anthony had come to her aid so quickly and kindly when she was wrongfully accused. He hadn't complained or expressed any negativity toward her, though he certainly had the right to.

*Did I truly apply my heart to understanding?* she wondered. Her decision to date Ty was seeming less and less wise.

Even though her friend Rachel was busy getting ready for her wedding the following day, she and Olivia had a heart-to-heart discussion for more than an hour that afternoon. They reminisced about their years as roommates and their two transfers together as missionary companions. In so many ways, Rachel and Olivia felt like sisters.

"My love for Eric has totally grown during our engagement," said Rachel. "He makes me feel loved and understood. When I'm feeling sad, which is more often than not, he's my shelter in the storm. Whenever he's struggling for some reason, I try to give him the same support and love that he needs."

"You'll be great together," Olivia said with a smile. "I'm really happy for you."

"I'm sure there will be misunderstandings," replied Rachel. "Marriage will be new to us. And we both can be kind of messed up in our own weird ways, but we've committed to always be kind to each other, even when we're tired or annoyed.

"Speaking of being messed up, last time we talked it seemed you were torn between dating Anthony and Ty. Which one did you choose?"

"I decided to date Ty, because I just need to close that chapter of my life. My wounds just haven't healed all the way yet. It was a tough decision. If it doesn't work out, I hope I can somehow start dating Anthony again. That is if he'll even take me back. I'm worried he's already moved on. I know I deeply hurt him."

"So, how's it going with Ty?"

"Pretty well. He seems like a new man. Really thoughtful and a much better listener. I know you had some concerns about him when we dated in Provo, but I wish you could see him now."

"Do you love him?"

"That's tough to say. I have my doubts about him. And the more I'm with him, the less certain I am. On my flight here, I thought about Anthony as much as I thought about Ty."

"There's something I think I should tell you," Rachel said, her tone becoming more serious. "It happened a long time ago, but you deserve to know about it."

A worried look clouded Olivia's face.

"Last April, at the end of winter semester, you went home for a couple weeks. While you were gone, Ty went out with a BYU law student several times. I know the girl because we had some classes together before she started law school. We were sitting in the cafeteria one day and Ty walked by. He stopped and said 'hi' to both of us. After he left, she told me that she'd gone out with him for six straight nights. They kissed several times, but then he never called her again. Totally ghosted her."

Olivia appeared skeptical. "I find that hard to believe."

"Why is it hard to believe? He ended things with you pretty much the same way. And I know this guy was definitely Ty. I know him when I see him. He actually greeted me by name when he saw me. But this happened almost a year ago. Maybe he *has* changed."

"Thanks for telling me," said Olivia. "That's good to know. But Ty would never pull something like that now."

"I hope you're right," Rachel said. "I just don't want you to get hurt again."

Olivia had an incredible time in Portland with Rachel. Although she never admitted it to her friend, she was hurt to learn that Ty had gone out with another girl while she'd been away. During that period of time, they'd agreed to date exclusively. She had kept her part of the agreement.

Apparently, Ty had not.

Since Olivia was going to be in Portland for three days, Ty had planned to spend extra time at the office catching up on things. By dinner time on Monday evening, however, he was ready to go home. There was still plenty of work to be done, but he was bored and wanted to catch a soccer game on TV. As he was leaving the office, he ran into Allison.

"You're working late tonight," he said.

"So are you," she replied. "I was helping organize some files, but I just finished."

He then surprised himself by saying, "What are you doing after this? Want to join me for dinner and a movie?"

She lit up. "I'd love to." She had been secretly hoping Ty would ask her out.

His invitation to Allison was purely spontaneous, but he'd always felt she was fun and attractive. He would be taking a small risk by going out with her while Olivia was away, but taking risks added spice to life. He and Olivia would soon be engaged. After that, he'd *never* go out with anyone else. But Allison was cute, and he didn't want to spend the next few nights alone in his apartment, or worse, at the office.

To reduce the chance of someone seeing them together, Ty chose a small restaurant off the beaten path. Their dinner went well. Allison was fun and happy and interesting. At the end of their evening, she invited Ty to dinner at her home the following night. Her parents were out of town and she recommended that he bring his swimming trunks so they could swim in her backyard pool.

Not only did Ty arrive at Allison's right on time for dinner, but he surprised her with a small bouquet of flowers. She then gave him a tour of the spacious home where she lived with her parents.

The dinner she prepared was heavenly.

"You're a wonderful cook," he said enthusiastically.

She smiled. "I've always loved to cook. Glad you like it."

"Tell me more about your family," he said while sitting by the pool.

"Let's see. Well, my mom and dad both grew up here and were high school sweethearts. I have three older sisters. My dad served a mission in Brazil. I served in Alaska. And my sister, Anne, served in England."

"What are your parents like?"

"My mom stays really busy with lots of different projects and church callings. She also takes care of my nieces and nephew quite often. My dad owns a bunch of sporting goods stores. He has a couple here in Savona Springs, plus some in Arizona and Nevada. Business is booming, which keeps him on his toes."

*Managing a sports store sounds like more fun and less stressful than being a lawyer*, Ty thought.

Allison launched off the diving board and landed in a cannonball. Ty laughed and jumped in after her. Next door, Fletcher Park's wife, Sarah, was working in her study. She had a panoramic view of the mountains to the east. Ty had no idea that Fletcher's family and Allison's family were neighbors and close friends. Soon after sunset, Sarah noticed Allison and a young man swimming together in the pool.

The next evening, Allison was again in the pool with the young man. As Fletcher and Sarah went to bed that night, she said, "It looks like Allison has a boyfriend. I saw them kissing in the pool tonight."

Near the end of the third evening they spent together, Ty felt that he needed to clear the air with Allison and let her know about Olivia. "There's something I should probably tell you," he said. "I'm sorry, but I should've told you this before. I'm kind of in another relationship right now. Within a few weeks, I'll know if it's going to work out with her or not. If it doesn't, I'd love to date you. I've really enjoyed being with you these last few nights. Honestly, it's been great."

Allison felt hurt and disheartened. It upset her that Ty had waited so long to tell her about his other relationship, but she was willing to forgive him because after just three dates, she was already falling in love.

# Chapter 29
## *A Matter of Trust*

Allison sat in the garage, frustrated and unsure of what to do next. Her car wouldn't start. In fact, it wouldn't even make a sound as she turned the key in the ignition. *Perhaps the battery got drained somehow*, she thought.

Normally, she'd ask her dad for help. But with him out of town, she felt like her trusted mechanic had abandoned her. Allison noticed Fletcher pulling out of his driveway next door, so she waved him down and asked for a ride to the office.

As they merged onto the highway, Allison said, "I've actually been on a few dates with one of the associates from the firm."

"Really? Which one?"

"Ty Bradwell."

Fletcher tried to hide his surprise. After all, Ty had told him that he was dating Olivia. "Do you like Ty?" he asked.

"Totally. He's fun. We had dinner on Monday night. Then he's come over to my house for dinner and to swim. There's just one problem. He told me that he's already in a relationship. I'm not sure what he's going to do, but he says that he really likes me."

*That's very interesting*, Fletcher thought.

On that same morning, Olivia arrived for work at The Melby Foundation. She tried to focus on her projects, but her thoughts kept drifting to the conversation she'd had with Rachel. The news that Ty dated someone else behind her back still troubled her. She took comfort in the fact that his misbehavior had happened almost a year ago. She'd seen Ty become more thoughtful than he ever was when they'd dated in Provo.

Her thoughts soon turned to Anthony. He was someone who would never betray her trust. He was loyal and kind, and he'd been extremely gracious toward her even though she spurned him for Ty.

Fletcher walked briskly from his office to the Melby Foundation building. It was a short jaunt of only two blocks.

First, Fletcher visited his good friend, Lee Melby. He expressed his admiration for the foundation's recent efforts to reduce the number of children killed or seriously injured in accidents.

"Does Olivia Michaels have an office in this building?" he then asked.

"Yes, you'll find her three doors to the left."

Olivia's office door was partially open, but Fletcher knocked anyway. "Remember me?" he asked.

"You're Mr. Parks of Parks & Lane, right?"

"That's me. There's something rather personal I would like to discuss with you."

Olivia was puzzled. She couldn't imagine what personal information Fletcher would want to share with her, but she knew Fletcher was Ty's boss.

"Let me start with some background. On Monday, I rode on the elevator with Ty. He told me that the two of you are dating seriously. He seemed happy you decided to stop dating Anthony Hull."

"Yes, we've been dating a while now. It's going well."

Fletcher then asked, "Have you been out of town this week?"

Olivia nodded. "I went up to Portland for my friend's wedding. Why?"

"I live next door to a wonderful family I've known for the past 10 years. They have a daughter who returned a few months ago from a mission in Alaska. I recently hired her to be the receptionist at our firm. She knows all of the attorneys at our firm, including Ty. Her name is Allison."

Olivia was puzzled. She had no idea where Fletcher was heading.

"This morning, I gave Allison a ride to work. She told me that for the past few nights she has been going out with your Ty. They've been having dinner at her house and going swimming in her pool."

"There must be some mistake," she said. "Ty and I are focusing on each other right now." But she knew in her heart that Fletcher was telling the truth. She'd only been gone for three days and Ty was already stepping out on her.

Olivia felt crushed and betrayed. She had previously decided not to bring up with Ty the fact that he'd dated another girl in Provo. It had

114

been a long time ago, after all. But now Fletcher was telling her that the new Ty was not so reformed after all.

"Do you think your neighbor and Ty might just be friends?" she asked softly, even though she already knew the answer.

"No, Allison told me that she is romantically interested in Ty. Also, I forgot to tell you one other detail. My wife saw them kissing in the pool multiple times."

Olivia was silent.

After a long pause, Fletcher said, "Last night, Ty told Allison that if his relationship doesn't work out with you, he wants to continue dating her."

Olivia eyes filled with tears. "Why are you telling me this? Why do you care?"

Fletcher looked kindly at her. "I care because you're a good person. I care because your grandfather Ezra is one of my clients. And I care because I have a daughter about your age. If she had a serious boyfriend who was dating someone behind her back, I'd want her to know about it."

"Well, thanks for telling me all of this," she said so softly that Fletcher could barely hear. "I needed to know the truth."

After Fletcher left, Olivia stayed glued to her seat. A feeling of betrayal poured over her. She thought about how she had asked Ty if she could go to the gala with Anthony, an idea Ty had firmly rejected. "We need to focus solely on each other," he'd said. "And Anthony won't have any trouble finding another date."

*What a hypocrite*, she thought.

Olivia realized she finally had the clarity she needed. She'd spent the necessary time with Ty to see who he really was. Now, she could end things on her terms—close the book and hopefully begin a whole new story with Anthony.

She promptly sent a text to Ty. "I won't be able to have dinner with you tonight. Could you come by my house around 8:00? We need to talk about something."

He soon responded. "Sure. I'll be there."

Olivia's thoughts turned to Anthony. *I love him and I trust him.* She felt an overwhelming desire to hear his voice. To tell him that she chose him with all her heart. Unfortunately, her call to him went to voicemail. "Please call me," she said. "I'd love to talk with you."

A few minutes later, she tried texting him, again without success.

As she waited for Anthony to reply, her thoughts turned to fond memories of him. She was touched by his friendship with the boy who had been paralyzed. She remembered how he brought flowers to Grandma Angela after the special Family Home Evening, and continued to forge a bond with her over the months. Most of all, she remembered the way he risked missing his own flight to save her trip to England when she was only a stranger.

Finally, her phone rang.

"Hi, Olivia. It's great to hear your voice again."

"I have some good news for you!" she exclaimed. "I hope it will make you happy."

Anthony was silent for several moments. He then said, "I'd love to hear the good news in person, if it's all the same to you. I can be at your office in about 20 minutes."

"Great. See you soon!"

Olivia greeted Anthony with a kiss and a warm hug. "I've finally gotten the clarity I needed. I'm breaking up with Ty tonight," she said. "I never want to see him again. Well, I'm going to see him for a few minutes tonight, but that's just to tell him that we're over." She paused. "I want you back, if you'll take me. I made a dumb decision to put our relationship on hold. It wasn't fair to you at all. Is there any way you can forgive me?"

Anthony smiled and said, "You don't need to ask for my forgiveness, and I'd love to have you back. I've missed you even more than I thought I would."

"I've missed you, too!" she said. "Ty is coming to my house at 8:00 tonight. It should only take about fifteen minutes to end things. Can you come over at 8:30?"

"I'll see you then. I love you."

They kissed once more.

She then smiled at Anthony and said, "You make me so happy!"

# Chapter 30
## *What a Difference a Zero Makes*

Later that afternoon, Fletcher met with a new client named Marilyn Johnson. Just as he'd predicted, she arrived 15 minutes early for her appointment. He had learned years ago that most elderly clients arrive early. They also tend to pay their bills ahead of schedule.

Once they were seated, Mrs. Johnson introduced herself by saying, "I'm an 88-year-old widow and I don't have a will. I think it's about time I got one. My brother speaks highly of you, so that's a good enough endorsement for me."

"What is your brother's name?"

"Ezra Harris."

Fletcher was surprised. "Ezra is a great man. I've really enjoyed working with him. I had a meeting with him last week and he seemed to be doing pretty well, but I spoke to his daughter this morning and she said he's now in a coma."

"Yes, I just heard that news myself. He probably has just a week or two left. Maybe less."

"I'm really sorry to hear that," Fletcher said.

"It's a punch to the gut, for sure. But don't worry too much about him. He's one of those people who's going straight to heaven.

"The reason I've been anxious to talk to you is that Ezra and I both sold some family land a couple of years ago. We each received $900,000, before taxes."

Fletcher was confused. "I would like to clarify something. You just said when you sold the land you inherited, you and your brother Ezra only got $900,000 each, before taxes."

"That's correct. We each got $900,000. But I don't think of it as *only* $900,000. That's a lot of money to me. And to most people, I'd expect. Just maybe not to a lawyer."

"That is absolutely a lot of money to me, too," Fletcher said apologetically. "I used the word 'only' because Ezra told me several times that when you sold your undeveloped land, you each received $9 million."

Marilyn laughed out loud. "I wish! No, we both got $900,000 before taxes. We owned just one acre of land each."

"These are crucial clarifications. I thought you and Ezra had much more land than that."

"No, it was one acre. I'll send you the closing documents."

"So, Ezra was off by just a zero, which was the difference between getting $9,000,000 and $900,000," Fletcher said. "Meeting with him, he always seemed pretty sharp and clear-headed for his age."

"He's usually quite sharp," Marilyn said. "But sometimes he can really get things confused. You should see him try to operate his DVD player. I once saw him trying to shove a book into it."

Later that afternoon, Marilyn sent a copy of the closing documents related to Ezra's land sale. The paperwork confirmed Ezra had owned just one acre of land and sold it for $900,000.

Fletcher called Ty and asked him to come to his office.

"I have some news about Ezra Harris," Fletcher said. "I met with his sister today. Ezra was seriously mistaken. He thought that he sold his land for $9 million, but it was actually $900,000. His total estate is now worth around $2 million. His will says the first $2.5 million goes to his only child, Mary. This essentially means that *everything* will go to Mary."

"So, Olivia and her brothers get no inheritance at all?" Ty asked in disbelief.

"That's right. Olivia gets no inheritance."

From the look in Ty's eyes, it was clear he was disappointed. But Fletcher saw something else brewing.

"I can't believe this," Ty said, shaking his head. His voiced harshened in anger. "I told you Ezra was losing it mentally. He was obviously confused, but you wouldn't listen. This is pathetic!"

Fletcher didn't immediately respond. He stared intently at Ty in silence.

Ty quickly realized that he'd crossed the line by criticizing his boss so forcefully. "I'm sorry," he said. "I let myself get too worked up."

"It's time for you to leave," said Fletcher.

"I'll go back to my office right now."

"I must not have made myself clear. What I'm saying is that it's time for you to leave this law firm. I told you that you were on a strict probation. The way you just treated me is unacceptable."

Ty was stunned. "I'm sorry I got upset. It won't happen again."

"The attorneys at this firm must have good judgment," Fletcher said firmly. "If you had good judgment, you wouldn't have criticized me today. You wouldn't have broken into my office and searched through my files. I'm disgusted by your behavior. The only reason I've kept you on this long was out of pity."

"Please don't fire me," begged Ty. "I really need this job."

"You should have thought about that before you acted unethically time and time again. You're a selfish young man and I seriously hope you can make changes in your life. I'm willing to do you one favor. Since it's a tough job market, we will give you three months' severance pay."

Ty relented. It was clear that Fletcher had made up his mind. And he didn't want to lose the generous offer of severance pay.

Still in a state of shock, Ty stood up to leave. His head felt heavy and his eyes began to sting. Slowly, he returned to his office to begin the process of cleaning out his desk and transferring his current projects to other attorneys.


Ty knocked on Olivia's door, unsure of what she wanted to discuss. Regardless of how their conversation was going to unfold, his interest in her was rapidly fading. Whether it was the lack of inheritance or just the passing of time, he found himself thinking more and more about Allison.

Olivia didn't waste any time getting to the point. "I know you haven't been truthful with me. I know you've dated other people behind my back. I honestly can't believe you'd treat me—or anyone—this way. It's just sad. But I'm not going to be a victim here. I'm moving on, Ty. I wish you all the best in life, but I don't ever want to see you again."

She expected Ty to flash his adorable smile and turn on the charm in an effort to change her mind. His lackluster reaction couldn't have surprised her more.

"You're right," he said. "I haven't been the best boyfriend. I haven't been much good at a lot of things lately. I'm sorry. You deserve better."

Olivia felt relieved. "I think it's time to say goodbye."

"I think so. Thanks for being such a good friend, Olivia. I'll always respect you."

They hugged briefly and then he was gone. Their tumultuous relationship had ended with a whimper. And after that final hug, neither Ty nor Olivia even made eye contact, as both were busy thinking about other people.

# Chapter 31
## *A Sudden Turn*

Anthony leaned back in his chair and surveyed the computer screen. He'd finally completed the five-page paper assigned by his Institute teacher. The topic was Joseph Smith's incarceration in the ironically named Liberty Jail.

Researching and writing the paper had given Anthony a deeper appreciation of the trials that Joseph and his fellow prisoners faced. They'd been unjustly confined in that dreary prison for more than four months, suffering in freezing temperatures with only meager amounts of food. The jailers sometimes even poisoned the food, causing the prisoners to violently vomit for days.

Anthony's next task was to complete a paper for his business class. As he looked through his notes, he realized he'd misread the instructions—the paper wasn't due until the following Friday. With this unexpected addition of free time, he decided to go on a hike in Prospector's Canyon since it was a beautiful day and Olivia wasn't expecting him until later that evening.

His heart had been filled with joy ever since he'd spoken with Olivia. The idea of being with her forever far outweighed any frustrations he felt from the past few weeks. He couldn't wait to see her again and start a new chapter together.

For the first 15 minutes of his drive up the canyon, Anthony saw very little traffic. He had no way of knowing that a 35-year-old man with two prior DUIs was speeding down the road in his truck. The man had been drinking all afternoon.

As Anthony rounded one of the canyon's sharpest turns, he was shocked to see a fast-moving truck barreling toward him on the wrong side of the road. He slammed on his brakes and yanked his steering wheel to the right, barely missing the truck.

He felt grateful that he'd avoided what seemed like a guaranteed collision. His car had come to rest on the road's dirt shoulder. It tilted slightly but felt as though it had come to a complete stop.

He breathed a sigh of relief. *That was too close*, he thought.

Suddenly, his car began to tilt. Then it started to roll. After several violent rotations, his car came to rest far below the canyon road. It was in a somewhat upright position. Because the roof of the car was severely dented, Anthony could not sit up straight.

His mind was spinning. Everything had happened so fast.

Anthony bowed his head and said a quick prayer, thanking his Father in Heaven that he hadn't been seriously hurt or killed. He was able to open the car door far enough to squeeze out. As he started to move his legs, he realized that his left foot was stuck. His lower left leg was entrapped by tangled metal. He couldn't even see his foot.

He felt sharp pain as he struggled to free his foot from the car's grasp. Taking a different approach, he put his hands around his left calf and twisted it back and forth, while also pulling upward. Once again, he felt a sharp pain, and his foot did not budge.

He felt like a wounded animal caught in a vicious trap.

His left foot throbbed. And it was increasingly wet. *It must be bleeding*, he thought. *I hope it's not too much. I should stop pulling so hard. I don't want to bleed to death.*

Anthony tried to carefully peel back the metal that surrounded his foot. He had some tools in his trunk that would make this task easier, but he had no way of getting to them.

He had told Olivia that he'd come over at 8:30 that evening. If he didn't show up, she'd most likely call him before too long. The problem was that Anthony's phone ended up on the floor of the back seat, next to the far passenger side door. He tried several times to reach it, but always came up a few inches short.

Other worries tormented him. He had several bottles of water and some granola bars, but they were what seemed like a million miles away in his trunk. Also, he couldn't start his engine, which meant that he'd have no heat at night. To make matters worse, his car's horn was no longer working, so he couldn't use it to attract the attention of others.

Anthony hadn't told anyone that he was going hiking in Prospector's Canyon. Even if Olivia reported him missing, people wouldn't know where to begin to look for him.

He recalled that a few years earlier, a woman had died in Prospector's Canyon after her car rolled down a steep embankment. It took searchers five days to find the woman because her car wasn't visible from the road. Looking out from the partially opened door of his car, Anthony couldn't see the canyon road above him.

*If I can't see the road, people on the road probably can't see me.*

Anthony reverently bowed his head to offer another prayer. His voice was trembling. *Please let me live so that I can marry Olivia. And please let me live so I can help my mom. Please inspire someone to find me.*

As the shadows lengthened and temperatures dropped, Anthony prepared himself for a miserable night. With no food, no water, and a leg wound that was still bleeding, he knew this would be a dangerous race against time.

# Chapter 32
## *Searching for Anthony*

Anthony still hadn't arrived at her house, and Olivia found herself pacing by the front window. He'd sounded so excited to see her and it was uncharacteristic of him to be so late. An hour had passed, and she'd called and texted multiple times.

No response.

*Where is he and why won't he answer?* she wondered.

After another 30 minutes, Olivia decided to call Anthony's mom.

"I can't get in touch with Anthony," she said. "He told me he'd be here almost two hours ago. Do you have any idea where he is?"

"I've been trying to reach him, too. He's not answering. This isn't like Anthony."

"I'm really worried," Olivia said softly.

"Are your parents home with you?" Stefanie asked.

"No, they're in New York at a medical convention. I'm here alone."

Fifteen minutes later, Stefanie showed up at Olivia's door. Olivia was grateful for her company and her support.

Stefanie decided it was time to contact the police. "I'm calling about my son, Anthony Hull. He has disappeared. Have there been any accidents tonight?"

"We've had a couple of minor fender-benders, but no accidents with any serious injuries," the officer said.

"Well, Anthony is late for a very important appointment. Something must be wrong."

The officer said, "If we get any information about your son, we'll let you know right away."

Olivia then called Anthony's best friend and teammate, Seth Jones. After explaining the situation, she enlisted his help. "Will you please make some calls to see if you can track him down, Seth? We have no idea where he could be."

"I'll get right on it," said Seth. He made at least a dozen calls. He also recruited others to reach out to Anthony, but no one was able to contact him.

Stefanie then suggested to Olivia that they seek assistance from a higher power. Stefanie offered a heartfelt prayer that could only come from a worried mother. When she finished, both women had tears in their eyes.

Throughout the night, Olivia called Anthony every 30 minutes. His phone always rang four times before going to voicemail. Feeling powerless, she also sent a barrage of text messages, hoping something would get through.

Little did she know that Anthony could hear each call and text. The alerts tormented him, as he still couldn't quite grasp his phone. It wasn't lost on him that this relatively tiny distance could very well be the difference between life and death.

He remembered reading about a man whose arm was pinned by a falling boulder in southern Utah. That man eventually had to cut off his arm with a knife to escape. In some ways, Anthony felt relieved he didn't have a knife within reach.

When Olivia tried to call Anthony early the next morning, his phone went straight to voicemail. She shook her head in frustration. *His battery must be dead. This can't be good.*

It had been a sleepless night for both Olivia and Stefanie. Distraught, scared, and emotionally exhausted, they'd offered many prayers together. They had wept and worried, but they still had no idea what had happened to Anthony.

# Chapter 33
## *Praying to Survive*

Never had a night dragged on so mercilessly for Anthony. Temperatures plummeted after the sun went down, and with no jacket, he shivered uncontrollably. His teeth began to ache from the violent chattering.

But Anthony was also facing a trial worse than the cold. A dark and deep loneliness had descended upon him. He couldn't find words to fully describe how helpless and alone he felt.

He bowed his head and prayed for comfort. He felt weak, so he also asked for strength. His overpowering loneliness soon returned. This cycle continued throughout the night. He would pray for relief and feel a measure of peace, but soon intense feelings of fear and loneliness would again overwhelm him.

*If only I could move my leg*, he thought. Being caught in a trap from which he could not escape made him feel powerless and claustrophobic.

Time dragged on. Even though he felt exhausted, he didn't sleep at all that night. His left foot throbbed with pain and he yearned for even one swallow of water. He'd never been so thirsty in his life. At least twice, he fainted.

He was also tormented by the thought that he might never see Olivia, his mom, and his other loved ones again in this life. Each time his phone rang, he pictured them in his mind. Even though he couldn't speak to Olivia and his mom, he still felt a brief connection with them. Eventually, the calls stopped.

Anthony's thoughts returned to Olivia. She must be terribly worried and frightened. He again regretted that he hadn't told anyone where he was going.

With all his heart, he knew he wanted to marry Olivia. He had great faith in the power of prayer, but knew not all prayers are answered in the way we want. Sometimes people die when they are still young, like Olivia's sister.

Anthony thought about all the things he admired about Olivia. Her kindness and her compassion. Her gift for seeing the good in others. Her sense of humor and optimistic nature. He loved the tenderness in her voice when she talked to him and the beauty in her voice when she sang.

How he wanted to hold Olivia in his arms and tell her how much he loved her. He wanted to walk through this life and the next with her by his side, hand-in-hand, together as one.

Anthony's heart also ached for his dear mom. He knew she'd be devastated by the unexplained disappearance of her only son. She had already endured tragic loss, and he desperately wanted to survive so he could be there to support her.

As the first traces of dawn finally lit the sky, Anthony felt as if he had been released from a deep, dark prison. He still felt lonely and thirsty, but the morning sun brought a glimmer of hope.

He decided to try again to release his foot from the grasp of the car. He squeezed his left calf with both hands and pulled hard. He screamed in pain, yet his foot didn't budge. He began speaking out loud, as it helped him feel less lonely.

"If I survive this, I want to learn more about Mom and show more interest in her. I've never asked her much about her high school and college years. I've never asked how Dad proposed to her. I want to be a better brother. And a better friend. I'll try to be more grateful and not take things for granted. I'll try to be more compassionate and look more for the good in others."

Anthony peered up at the sky and saw a majestic eagle soaring high above him. It reminded him of the eagle he'd seen on his first hike with Olivia. She had quoted a passage from Isaiah. Anthony had gone home that same night and memorized the passage. It had become a scripture that he thought about often.

The eagle passed from view, but the bright beauty of the sky remained. Anthony recited the verse aloud. "But they that wait upon the Lord shall renew their strength; they shall mount up with wings as eagles; they shall run, and not be weary; and they shall walk, and not faint."

For the first time since his accident, Anthony felt peace. He wasn't as weary as he'd been during the night. Although he was still exhausted, he somehow felt stronger.

Anthony heard a clatter in the distance and stared up the embankment. Two policemen were approaching his car. He wasn't sure if he were dreaming or not. Still, Anthony smiled and gave the policemen two thumbs up.

Earlier that morning, a girl had spotted Anthony's car while she was bird watching. She promptly called the police.

As the officers worked to release his left leg from the car, paramedics arrived. Ten minutes later, he was free. They placed Anthony on a stretcher and carried him up to the road, where the ambulance was waiting. He gave his mom's phone number to a police officer, and as paramedics started an IV, he begged the man to call and let her know he was okay.

When the call came, Stefanie placed it on speakerphone so Olivia could also listen. "Your son is on his way to Lakeside Hospital. His car rolled off Prospector Canyon road. He has several nasty cuts and I think he might have a broken ankle, but he's going to be okay."

Stefanie and Olivia both wept as they hugged each other. After they knelt in a prayer of thanksgiving, they went straight to the hospital.

About 40 minutes later, a doctor appeared. "Are you Anthony's relatives?" he asked.

"Yes, I'm his mom."

Olivia then said, "I'm his fiancé."

Stefanie raised her eyebrows and smiled.

"I've got good news," the doctor said. "Anthony has no broken bones. He had a couple of gashes that required stitches. He was severally dehydrated, but he's been on an IV since the ambulance picked him up. He's already feeling a lot better. Give us five more minutes and then you can come see him. He's in room 215."

After five minutes had passed, Olivia said, "Mothers first."

Stefanie gave Olivia a hug. She then walked to Room 215, where Anthony was lying in bed. He began sobbing as soon as he saw her. She bent over and gave him a long, sweet hug. She was now crying, too.

"I was so frightened," she said. "I thought we were going to lose you, but here you are, safe and sound. I am so happy. I love you and I need you."

"Don't worry, mom. I'll always be here for you."

"There's someone else who wants to see you," his mom said. "I'll go get her."

When Olivia entered the room, she didn't say a word. She just smiled and walked toward his bed. He saw love in her eyes. She then bent over and gently kissed him on the lips.

"I can't believe how much I love you."

"I love you, too," he said warmly.

She then kneeled down on one knee and said to Anthony, "Will you marry me?"

"I thought you'd never ask," he replied with a smile.

# Epilogue

Two months after Anthony's accident, he and Olivia were married in the San Diego Temple. They had only recently returned from their honeymoon when he was hired as an assistant basketball coach at Savona Springs University.

Not long afterward, Ty married Allison, the swimming receptionist. He wasn't selected as "Mr. Truly Blue," but the agency promised to keep his headshots on file. Ty was now working as an assistant manager at one of the sporting goods stores owned by Allison's dad. They lived in her parents' spacious basement and often went swimming in the outdoor pool.

The following year, Olivia gave birth to identical twin daughters. The first baby to arrive was named Bella. The second was named Angela.

After the babies were blessed, Grandma Angela's health started going downhill. Olivia and Anthony went to see her. Although she was weak, her mind was still clear.

Tears ran down Olivia's cheeks as she gently took her grandma's hands. "Thank you for being such a wonderful example. You have been a shining light in my life. You've helped guide me through so much. I love you with all of my heart."

In a faint voice, Angela said, "Treat each other like a treasure."

She then was silent.

Although Anthony did not hear it, Olivia clearly heard her grandma whisper, "Always."

And then she was gone, but never forgotten.

# ABOUT THE AUTHOR

Thomas Kelly holds degrees from Brigham Young University and Harvard Law School. He has practiced law for 30 years and cofounded JetBlue Airways. He has served in the Church of Jesus Christ of Latter-day Saints as a bishop, stake president, and president of the Italy Rome Mission. He and his wife, Kathy, enjoy spending time with their growing family of 10 children and 12 grandchildren.

This book is a fictional work, though many aspects of the story are drawn from Tom's life experiences.

Made in the USA
Lexington, KY
10 December 2019